THE SCIENCE OFFICER

VOLUME 1

BLAZE WARD

The Science Officer
Volume 1
Blaze Ward
Copyright © 2014 Blaze Ward
All rights reserved
Published by Knotted Road Press
www.KnottedRoadPress.com

ISBN: 978-1-64470-021-1

Cover art:
Copyright © Philcold | Dreamstime.com - Exploring Far Planets Photo

Cover and interior design copyright © 2014 Knotted Road Press

Never miss a release!
If you'd like to be notified of new releases, sign up for my newsletter.

I will never spam you, or use your email for nefarious purposes. You can also unsubscribe at any time.

http://www.blazeward.com/newsletter/

The Doomsday Vault

The Last Flagship

The Hammerfield Gambit

The Hammerfield Payoff

Doyle Iwakuma Stories

The Librarian

Demigod

Greater Than The Gods Intended

Other Science Fiction Stories

Myrmidons

Moonshot

Menelaus

Earthquake Gun

Moscow Gold

Fairchild

White Crane

***The Collective* Universe**

The Shipwrecked Mermaid

Imposters

BOOK ONE: PIRATES

PART ONE

Javier quickly scanned the boards on his bridge console, on the off-chance that an asteroid was on an intercept course. The jump drives would require another hour to recharge after this latest hop, and the engines were off-line for now as the computer worked out a preliminary scan of the new system they were here to survey.

Space was really, really big. The odds of any two objects intersecting accidentally were extremely low. Like, lots of zeros behind the decimal low. But always followed by a one. Javier never forgot that. Eventually, your number would come up. Hopefully it would be old age that got you, though, instead of a jealous boyfriend.

The immediate area, out to around half a light-second, was clear. In the distance, a dim reddish-orange sun fought fitfully to warm the neighborhood. Just another boring star system on the far side of beyond. Another day, another *drachma*.

"Suvi. Mission log," Javier said, keying the computer system live with his voice. It wasn't really a she, and she wasn't really intelligent, but the AI was a pretty good facsimile of a person. And he had tweaked her programming over the years to get her just right.

The fleet hadn't bothered with a name for the little vessel. They never did with probe-cutters. Scouts like this one usually just had hull numbers. After Javier had bought her from the wrecker yard, he had named the vessel *Mielikki*, after the Finnish Goddess of the Forest. He had reprogrammed the AI to appear as a petite Anglo woman, an elfin blue-eyed blond, and named her Suvi. *Summer*. It was a nice contrast to his own dark hair and dark skin. Reminded him that the galaxy was a big place filled with all sorts of strange humans.

"Go ahead, Javier," Suvi replied crisply. She appeared on a side screen as if she was sitting in an office on an old warship, dressed in a uniform vaguely modeled on a fleet yeoman from a century ago, just before the Great Wars broke out. Javier was positive the AI hadn't originally been programmed with a sense of irony and humor, but, looking at her attire, she had developed one over time.

"Mission day 237, newly arrived and scanning. Tag this as part of Campeche Sector, system number seven," he said, bringing up a holographic star map of the neighborhood. "Sometime in the next two or four systems, we'll transition to Quintana Roo Sector, before we hit the edge of the local arm and enter a gulf. Please remind me."

"Will do, Javier," she replied, appearing to type something on a keyboard in front of her.

"Very good, Suvi. You have the deck. I'll be in back getting some food and checking the botany station." Javier unbuckled, rose from his chair, and made his way aft. He stretched his arms overhead and tugged his tunic back down into place after he scratched an itch by his kidney.

Behind him, the beaming elf took charge. "Roger that, Captain."

JAVIER PLUCKED a second berry from the bush as he carefully spit out the first seed into his hand. The berry was almost the size of a grape, but shockingly pink and very sweet. Javier smiled at what he'd been able to accomplish with a full research lab and several years of solitary patience. He might have invented another new species of fruit. One of these days, he needed to go visit some parish fair back home, just so he could win all the ribbons for fruits and vegetables. Maybe.

Around him, *Mielikki's* original cargo hold had been split into two pieces. The interesting half was now dedicated to botanical research, with a small arboretum, fruit and vegetable patches, a hydroponics rig with several species of fish, and a seed library better than many agricultural universities maintained.

Fleet Operations had laughed when he demanded real Ukrainian dirt from the homeworld, rich and black, but had shipped him out nearly fifty cubic meters of the stuff as part of his contract. On his side trips back to "known" space, admirals and legates were always quite happy to have fresh picked grapes, or blood oranges, or blue asparagus to serve with dinner.

For now, Javier pulled one of the small bags from his pocket, kept for just this purpose, and added the seed from his hand. He placed the sealed bag in a netting shelf nearby and pulled out a clear box for the berry. That went into a small refrigerator, until it could be scanned, cataloged, and planted in a fresh pot, to see which way grew better, naked seed or buried fruit. Ah, science.

A sound attracted Javier's attention. He glanced over as Athos, one of his chickens, emerged from the vegetable patch and cocked her head at him. She stared at him for a moment longer, decided there wasn't going to be any food, and went back to scratching in the dirt for anything interesting to eat.

Javier smiled and took a really deep breath. He sighed. Most of the planets he had visited didn't have air this clean and fresh, to say nothing of warships that kept amenities to a minimum, or sector stations that didn't even bother with that. Fresh water, clean air, and no people. This was paradise.

"Captain to the bridge," came the sudden interruption. Suvi's voice was poised and calm. "Emergency. All hands to battle stations."

FOURTEEN YEARS as a *Concord* Fleet officer had left its mark. Javier covered the distance to the command room almost before the echoes of her voice had faded.

Even before his butt hit the chair, he was assessing screens. "Suvi. Status report," he called as he brought his boards live and considered his options.

The probe-cutter boats had been armed when commissioned, but *Mielikki* had had most of that stripped when she was turned into a long-range scout. Sure, there was still a little twin-pulsar in a dorsal turret, but that was mainly useful against unexpected asteroids in tight quarters. Javier reached for the armaments console, and then stopped when he saw the image on the secondary screen.

"Crap," he said quietly. "Where did she come from?"

The hull displayed was a flat charcoal gray shark so dark as to almost be almost black. Even at a range Javier could call knife-fighting, the vessel was hard to see. The scanners, however, showed her just fine. Now.

"Working," came the response, even though the AI was much faster than that. "She appears to have been cloaked and nearby when we arrived. The vessel appears to be a…"

"She's an Osiris-class heavy corvette," he cut her off mid-word.

Javier knew the class. He still remembered many midshipman cruises at the *Concord* Academy on Bryce aboard the old *Bannockburn*, one of this one's sisters. He was out-gunned by orders of magnitude, and couldn't possibly run away from the fast vessel. And the jump engines wouldn't be online for another twenty minutes. He was right proper screwed.

"Suvi," he said, face twisted up in a sideways scowl, "have they hailed us?"

Her image showed fierce concentration. "Negative. No wait, stand by." She paused, a look of incredulous shock growing on her face. "Oh, my…"

The image on the screen was ancient, dating back to the distant past, when humans were confined to a single homeworld and ships floated on water instead of sky. A human skull, white on a black background, with crossed thigh bones behind.

Javier had just enough time to realize that the flag was black instead of red, and then the vessel opened fire.

Darkness.

Utter silence.

Something bumped him on the head.

Javier blinked.

The emergency backup lighting came on.

Javier was floating. The bump was the ceiling.

Crap. Grav plates were off.

Mielikki was dead in the water.

Of course. They were pirates. They had ionic pulsars. One overwhelming surge of static later, and every system on

Mielikki was overloaded. It would take three hours to reset all the breaker boards and bring everything back on line at this point. He probably had three minutes. *Needs must, when the devil drives.*

Javier pushed off from the ceiling, moving through the air like a porpoise.

Emergency lifesuit first. Unarmored. Barely reinforced. Keep him alive if they blew the airlocks out.

Forty-seven seconds. Some skills never faded.

Computer next. He held the console with one hand and climbed underneath to access a panel. It wasn't the computer core. That was down in the bowels near the power systems. He just wanted his logs, and Suvi's personality files, intact.

Javier swapped the fifth chip from the left for a spare his fleet-trained paranoia kept taped close by. With Suvi tucked into his pocket, he smashed the blank replacement with a small hammer, as well as all the rest of the chips and boards. Standard procedure when about to be captured, although he was supposed to destroy the chip with data, not try to smuggle it past the enemy. Tough. He liked Suvi. Now, to hide her.

Javier checked the clock in his head. Two minutes gone.

He dove headlong down the main corridor to the veterinary station, which was a very fancy term for a chicken coop and examination table. He cracked a feed bucket open just enough to slide Suvi in and then latched it back down.

There was amazingly little debris floating around. Fourteen years active duty, four years Academy, and several years of private space flight will do that to you.

The chickens didn't mind zero gravity. Well, they minded, but they were chickens. Everything offended them. They didn't appear to be much bothered. Another couple of hours and they'd probably prefer to live in a place where their wings worked.

He might have to try that as an experiment someday. *The Effects of Minimal Gravity from Birth on Terran Chicken Breeds*. Javier snorted at the thought of a research journal article. Pirates first. Tenure later.

The whole ship rang like a bell.

Time's up.

Javier considered the personal sidearm he kept in his cabin. That would just get him killed quickly. Talking seemed to offer the only chance of getting out of this alive. Not much, but better than sure death.

He moved to the main corridor and set his radio to scanning for frequencies in use.

It didn't take long. They were on a default fleet channel.

"Greetings," he said. "Can we talk?"

Javier waited patiently. Everyone had gone silent as soon as he spoke. He let them talk on another channel for a few moments before he went looking for it.

"Hello," he said, interrupting a man and a woman talking.

"Who is this?" challenged the male voice. Gruff, hard, professional. It reminded him of one of his instructors from his Academy days.

"The guy on the ship," Javier replied, careful to keep his tone light and friendly. Never antagonize people with guns pointed at you. "Since you didn't blast me, you don't want me dead. I figured I'd try to make this a little easier, so you don't have to shoot me when you open the hatch."

A drop of flop sweat rolled down his nose, right at the point he couldn't get to it inside his helmet. Javier scrolled the lifesuit controls down as cold as it would go. Every little bit would help at this point. No fear in front of killers.

There was an awkward pause.

"How many people are on the ship?" The man's voice was calmer now. "And what cargo are you carrying?"

Javier shrugged to himself. They were going to find out in about five minutes anyway. "Me," he said. "Oh, and four chickens. As for goods, I'm hauling a lot of trees and plants."

"Trees?" the woman's sudden voice was incredulous. Harsh, cold, and vicious, but also incredulous. "What do you mean, trees?"

Javier smiled, swallowed it before responding. "Apple trees," he said, matter of fact. It was a speech he gave at almost every station and sector headquarters. "Pears, oranges, figs, bananas, cherries, hazelnuts, cashews, almonds. Bunch more. Plus fruit bushes, vegetables, hydroponics. And four chickens."

More silence.

She was not mollified. "That's bullshit," she said. "This is a patrol cutter."

Javier took a breath before he responded. "This is a probe-cutter, retired from active duty twenty years ago, and converted to a long-range survey scout."

The man's voice was back. "Who are you?"

Javier shrugged in his suit. "Just a guy on a survey contract for *Concord* Fleet. A private contractor trying to make a buck."

"And all the botany?"

Javier perked up a bit. These people didn't sound like pirates. At least not the ones in the shows or movies. Way too articulate for what he was expecting. "Hobby," he said. "Something to do when I spend two to three years at a time in the middle of nowhere."

Javier could hear the banging on the hatch in front of him. The airlock was about to be opened. With the ship powerless, they had already overridden the airlock bearings and cut the interlocks. And done it faster than most shipyard crews could manage. Damn. They were good.

The woman's voice was back now. She sounded angry.

Like a cat denied a mouse. "I've got you on my scanner," she said. "Where are your weapons?"

Javier shrugged. Things were about to get tricky. "I have a pistol in my cabin," he said. "Didn't figure it would do me much good here."

"You got that right, mister," she snarled. "You stand perfectly still when the lock opens. If you're lying about anything, you're a dead man."

Javier braced his foot under a rail put there by the ship's architect for exactly this situation. For good measure, he held his hands straight out sideways, open and as unthreatening as he could. "Got it."

The airlock door crawled open about eight centimeters, about as far as someone without gravity could torque it manually in one twist. Someone fantastically strong. Someone really angry.

A barrel poked through, like a hunting snake. No head appeared in the gap, so Javier assumed a camera on the gunsight.

He remained still. He even smiled. "Hi there."

"Don't move."

"Not planning to."

The hatch creeped farther open.

Somebody on the other side stuck a sensor pod across the threshold. It pinged loudly in the silence.

Nothing.

Javier wasn't used to meeting other people as patient as he was. He had expected them to come barging in shooting by now. Maybe this was a good sign.

The sensor pod chirped.

Javier slowly let out a breath he hadn't been aware he was holding. There was air, so they weren't going to blow the locks and vent his ship into space. Maybe another good sign.

A head appeared in the gap, over the barrel.

"Just you, huh?" It was her.

Javier nodded. "And four chickens."

The edge of anger in her voice was subsiding to exasperation. "What is it," she said, "about the damned chickens?"

Javier held his voice as steady as possible, even when it really wanted to go up an octave. "Some people eat chickens," he said, "and they are quite tasty. But they also make eggs if you treat them right. That means a meal every day for years, instead of one meal and done. I'd rather you not shoot my chickens. Kinda impossible to replace out here."

She swam forward across the threshold, like a Nereid moving in water. The barrel seemed centered on Javier's chest with magnets.

He could see her eyes through the filtered faceshield, barely. He felt like a rabbit confronting a bobcat. He smiled. "Hi."

And then she shot him.

PART TWO

Darkness.

Sensation.

Pain.

Wakefulness.

Javier opened his eyes slowly. Even the dim light hurt.

He settled for a squint.

"Gah. What is that putrid stench?" Javier's eyes came fully open, in spite of the brightness. His stomach would have climbed out of his mouth if there was anything in it. Small victories.

He tried to move. And found his hands were bound behind his back.

"Blood and martyrs," he continued, "don't you people know how to program a bio-scrubber?"

A hand cracked the side of his skull. Open palm, sharp but not damaging. "Mind your tongue."

Javier turned to look up at his tormentor. And kept looking up.

He was pretty sure it was a she, because she seemed to have breasts. Small ones, to be sure, hiding on top of muscles. Lots of muscles. And the bones in the face appeared female. Not particularly delicate. Definitely not feminine.

Brown hair worn short to fit inside a lifesuit, buzzed very short on the sides and spiked into a petite Mohawk. The only thing petite about her.

The only vaguely-female touch was the collection of rings, studs, and stones in both ears. Nothing through the nose, though.

And the voice was a studied alto. Sharp, crisp, forceful. Reminded him of a PT instructor from the Academy. The one who liked to sing on twenty mile hikes in full gear. He disliked her already.

Javier's eyes finally focused. Not that bad looking, though. If you liked them 2.1 meters tall and built like rugby players. And scowling.

Javier was having enough trouble not retching to be faux-polite. "Then stop trying to poison me and get me some clean air to breath, lady."

The hand came up again. Javier braced internally for the blow.

"Sykora, enough." The voice cut her off. She looked to her right, scowled, and subsided.

Javier processed the words. Slowly. Eventually. Heavy stun was like waking up still drunk the next morning, fifty kilometers from home, in someone else's clothes. Wearing clown shoes. Been there, done that.

He turned back to the voice and realized he was sitting in a small office, staring at a man behind a desk. An average-looking man. Shaved head where Javier kept his black hair comfortably long. Salt and pepper Vandyke, neatly trimmed where Javier was generally clean-shaven. Average build, average height. So close to Javier's 1.8 meters that they might see eye to eye. That would probably be important.

The man studied him, just as closely. "What do you

know about programming bio-scrubbers?" He held a mug of something warm and probably caffeinated. Javier noticed a big, heavy gold ring on his hand holding the mug. The kind you got from the Academy on Bryce when you graduated. And became an officer in the *Concord* Fleet. Huh.

Javier bit back the first rude thought that sprang to mind. Rugby girl would just hit him again. Or worse. "Have you been on my ship yet?"

The man's dark eyes got a guarded look. "I have not," he said. The voice was a rich baritone. Javier could hear the command tones underneath it. This was a man who was used to being in charge, and could pull it off.

Javier leaned forward a bit, until *her* hand landed on his shoulder and *planted* him into the chair. Damn. She might outweigh him, too. "Go smell the air over there and get back to me," he said. "Mind you, stay away from the bee hives and try not to torment the chickens any more than you have to, but go smell how nice my ship is, compared to this poisonous swamp of a death trap you're sailing in, Mister." Javier added the whip-crack to his voice they had both learned on Bryce.

He was rewarded by the man's glance down at where his hands would be, if they weren't tied behind him. Looking for The Ring. It was a rite of passage in the wider universe. Academy graduates. Strangers in strange lands.

The man leaned back and smiled, just a touch. Obviously, the same thoughts had crossed his mind. "I didn't see your ring, Mister." Yup, the universal greeting. Long-lost brothers-in-arms.

Javier shrugged, on firmer ground, if no safer. "My second wife kept it when she divorced me," he said. "Class of '63."

The man nodded, an entire silent, exquisite conversation. "I see. Class of '49." He turned to the woman hovering nearby, her weight just a suggestion now on Javier's shoulder. "Your observations, Sykora?"

Javier noticed her nails. Perfectly manicured, if kept extremely short. Again, working all the time in a lifesuit. He checked her wrist and saw the telltale calluses from an armored suit, the reinforced kind you wore when wrangling heavy equipment in zero-g, or heading into combat. She didn't look like an asteroid miner. Too tall.

She locked eyes with him for a second, as if reading his mind. Not that it was much deeper than a mud puddle, according to both his ex-wives. He winked at her. Her scowl deepened.

"He is correct, Captain," she said. "The ship is extremely clean and well kept. Well-founded, according to the engineering team, although the maintenance logs were destroyed when he smashed the personality computer."

The man, the Captain, scowled at Javier when he looked back. "Along with all the calibration records for the sensors and jump-drives?"

Javier just goggled at the man. "Hey," he said, "You people are pirates. SOP, buddy. Deal with it."

Sykora back-handed him, more of a love-tap than a blow. She growled under her breath.

The Captain tapped his finger, hard, on the desktop, to bring her up short. She glared at Javier anyway. If looks could kill.

Javier decided to ignore her. "So, Captain," he said, "what can I help you with?" He resisted leaning back and kicking his feet out. That might just get him killed.

The Captain glowered at him. Javier could see why he was the Captain when he turned all that charisma on. Power. Presence. The eyes got serious, piercing. The eyebrows flexed like muscles and moved together just a little, like they were pointing at him. Javier felt the man's whole presence centered on him. The voice sounded like a tool, or a weapon. Perfectly crafted, razor sharp, elegant.

"You could fix your highly-automated and customized ship so we could use it. Otherwise, we'll have to part it out and decide if you should be sold into slavery or just killed out of hand. What's your preference?"

Let's see. Lose, lose, or lose. A whole handful of bad choices. Kinda like how both marriages ended up. "How about I fix your bio-scrubbers and then you drop me someplace civilized so I can hitch-hike home? A way to say *thank you?*" Nobody every appreciated his ability to find silver linings.

The Captain was not amused. "Throw him in the brig for a while. Maybe he'll reconsider."

Javier watched, amazed, as Sykora picked him up out the chair, bodily, with one hand and sat him on his feet. "Gladly," she sneered.

Outside in the hallway, the air was even worse. Javier felt like he could walk on it. "How do you people breathe this *squamph?*" He coughed a few times, but that just sucked the crud deeper into his lungs instead of clearing them out.

Sykora didn't help matters. She grabbed him by the wrists behind his back and levered them up until he was on his knees. Through the pain in his shoulders, he did notice that the position compressed things enough that he stopped coughing. Probably not her original plan. Silver linings.

She lifted him again bodily by the scruff of the neck, and shoved him ahead of her. "Move, punk."

He glanced back. "If my ship's dead, can you put me in a cabin over there so I can at least breathe?"

That was good for a cuff to the side of the head. Not enough to rattle anything loose, just enough to shut most people up. Most people.

"Seriously," Javier said, looking over a shoulder, "can I at least fix yours if I have to breathe this gunk? I promise that clean air will make you a nicer person."

His first wife used to give him that same look. Uncanny.

She grabbed him by the collar to halt him, pushed a button to open a hatch, and casually shoved him through, bouncing him off the far bulkhead.

After a few of the stars faded from sight, he looked over a shoulder. "Handcuffs off, please?"

She glared down at the top of his head. "Face the wall," she growled.

Javier stood perfectly still when she unlocked him, and clenched a little as he expected a rabbit punch or another shot to the head, but she stepped back and activated the security field without a word.

Javier leaned close enough to the force field that it started to spark at him. "Remember, Sykora," he called, "clean air and smiling faces." He looked around, found a bed to sit on, and stretched out to contemplate his day.

Kinda sucky, but it could have been much, much worse.

THE VOICE JARRED him out of his daydreams. Probably just was well. They weren't fit for polite company anyway.

"On your feet."

Javier smiled. His princess Sykora had come back to rescue him. Or shoot him. Never a dull moment in space.

He stood up and stayed well back from the security field as she disarmed it and stepped to the doorway. She had to duck to clear the lintel. Javier maybe came up to her chin.

"Hands together in front," she said as she held out a set of manacles. Which was better than a pistol. He put his hands out politely and watched her cuff them expertly.

She pulled the connecting chain until he was almost

touching her chest, staring up into her face, which was probably a smarter response than sticking his nose between her boobs. Probably. "Come with me," she said, so quietly as to be almost a whisper.

Like I had a choice? Javier thought to himself. Even four years of Academy training in close-combat drill would make him look like a fool if he tried something. This woman was a killer. She pulled him into the hallway.

Sykora stood him up in front of a tall, skinny, Asian guy. Almost the same skin tone as his, but a different hue. He looked almost as confused as Javier. "Yu, this is…" She paused and stared hard at Javier. "What is your name, anyway?"

Javier stuck both manacled hands out at the man to shake. "Javier Aritza," he said with a smile. Silver linings. Yu shook absently.

"Aritza," she said, tense, "you are going to show Machinist's Mate Yu here how to fix the life-support system and tune the bio-scrubbers."

Javier looked up at her and blinked. "Or?"

She smiled cruelly. "Or I bounce you off the wall for a bit."

He smiled back, warm and sarcastic. "Didn't think I was your type, madam."

Light.

Pain.

Stars.

The wall was cold on his back. And his butt. And he was on the floor. And his face hurt where she had punched him. And his head had a goose egg growing where his skull had bounced off the bulkhead. And bells.

Wonderful. Another concussion. He hated getting concussions.

You felt like you were standing three feet behind yourself

and a little to one side, watching everything like it was happening to someone else.

Remote. Hard to process things in real time. Another really bad drunk. Punch drunk. The worst kind.

Javier kinda fish-eyed her as she grabbed him by the front of his tunic and hefted him upright. She looked closely at his face. He might have even talked, although nothing really coherent was going on behind his eyes, either.

Hallway.

Corridor lights.

Pretty music, but that might have been in his head.

Med-bay.

They were the same on every ship in space. Maybe one factory built them all and just slapped on different name plates.

Small room. Three meters by five. Two beds. One big console between them with robotic spider/waldo examination arms that did stuff to whoever you dropped onto the bed.

Javier found himself on his side on the port-side bed. Hands were still manacled.

Cold, proby thingee stretched out.

Bright light in each eye.

Cold something on the back of his head to make the bad go away.

Sting in the shoulder when the spider/waldo thingee bit him.

That was rude.

Oh.

Warm.

Happy thoughts.

Binary chemicals achieved medical significance.

Conscious thought.

Javier sat up with the fading remains of a bad hangover.

Or something. Four minutes had passed. She was still there, glowering. With the other guy. You-something?

Javier blinked.

Blinked again.

They were both still there.

"Ow. Was that necessary?"

She leaned in extra close. Even leered. Someone had been chewing wintermint gumdrops. "Necessary, Aritza? No. Fun? Absolutely. Feel free to keep mouthing off to me. Medbay's not far away, as long as I don't do anything the med-bot can't fix before you bleed to death."

Javier tried to concentrate on the freckle on the left side of her nose. Kissing her suddenly at this moment, as much fun as the look on her face would be, would probably get him killed. "I will try," he finally said, with some modicum of normalcy, "to keep that in mind. Where were we?"

He was almost back to competent when she pulled him off the bed and propelled him back into the hallway. Silver linings.

ENGINEERING on the old Osiris-class heavy corvettes was mainly on C deck, with a secondary-level catwalk down on B deck following the curve of the lower hull and allowing an awkward access to engineering spaces. The whole thing appeared to have been designed by circus contortionists who wanted to stay in practice while on duty.

Javier followed the skinny Asian guy through internal airlocks, with Sykora's hand heavy on his shoulder. She was holding him upright while he wobbled forward, as much as keeping him from running away.

Honestly, where did she think he was going to go?

The equipment on C-deck made his heart sink. The

Osiris boats were a bad tradeoff to begin with, adding guns and armor to a design that would have been better off with bigger engines to run away from capital ships. Someone had decided to fix that here. But they did it by adding a couple of auxiliary power reactors, one of which seemed to be bolted down exactly where you wanted to be sitting to work on the environmental systems.

Javier considered teaching the engineering crew new swear words, but he decided they probably already knew most of them, if they had to keep this mess running.

Javier watched Yu flag down a petite woman wearing the uniform of the Balustrade Imperial Navy, deepest green with yellow piping. "Chief, we're back."

The short woman kept her red hair medium length. Javier looked closer and realized she must have come from a high-gravity world originally. She wasn't squat, but had a perfectly proportioned body that had been stretched sideways and hung over heavy bones. Not bad, she only came up to his nose, and even then she might have out-weighed him.

She never glanced up at them from her portable computer and appeared to process the situation by reading their shadows on the deck plates. "That's good, Yu," she said diffidently. She glanced up for the briefest moment, studied Sykora. "Will it be safe to have him in here, Dragoon Sykora?"

Javier heard her voice right in his ear. "I'll keep close watch on him, Chief." He felt her pinch his shoulder to drive the point home. As if he was likely to forget.

They moved down a ladder/stairwell to B-deck. Yup. Just as bad as it looked from above.

Javier took a deep breath and turned to the guy. "We're gonna need a triage camera, a number four toolkit, and as many towels as you can scrounge up."

The man looked at him with concern and confusion. "What's a triage camera?"

Javier counted to five in his head. He'd already had one concussion today. "How long," he asked, wincing already in his mind, "have you been a Machinist's Mate, Yu?"

The man lit up. "Oh, I haven't passed the exam yet, sir," he smiled. "I've been an apprentice for four months now."

Javier nodded sagely. This was the way he got another punch in the face. He turned to the giantess. "And you're sure you won't let me in there to do this?"

Her smile was way too pleased with herself. "Absolutely," she purred. "Shall I tell Captain Sokolov you refused to help?"

One. Two. Three. Four. Five. "Will you hold the portable computer with the schematics loaded while I yell across the room?" Javier knew what refusal would buy him at this point. "And if we're gonna do brain surgery by remote control, can I have a comfy chair?"

In response, Sykora pushed him to the deck and leaned him against the bulkhead. "This looks comfy." She did at least pull out a portable computer and flip on the three-dee projector.

Javier reached into the beam and flipped the schematic projection around to face him. He sighed.

"Okay, Yu," he started. "After you remove the six bolts holding the primary panel in place, we'll need to disable the through-put and drain the primary system. You'll be looking for a blue pipe and a manual cutoff valve…"

<hr>

JAVIER WIPED the sweat from his forehead with both wrists still manacled together. At least he wasn't completely covered in muck and grime like Yu was. And how a black Norwegian rat ended up dead and wedged in the transverse coolant well might end up being one of those mysteries he wanted to ask God about when he died. But the machine was finally working.

He tried to stand, found that his feet, legs, and butt were asleep. He made it about halfway up the wall when he started to tumble over. Sykora nearly dislocated his shoulder when she jerked on the chain.

"Give it a rest, lady," he snarled, forgetting where he was in his tired state.

Sykora was quick to remind him. She grabbed him by the throat with her other hand and spiked him to the bulkhead hard enough to make his skull ring. Again. Yu sidestepped and just kind of stood there with a shocked look on his face as Sykora leaned close.

For a moment, just a moment, Javier considered biting her. It had already been enough of a day. Maybe things should go out with a bang.

"What did you say, punk?" she whispered. She was close enough to kiss, but Javier was dog-tired and cranky. She was close enough for a swift kick, too.

He took a deep breath. "I said I'm tired. I need a shower, a meal, and a nap. Your damned machine is fixed. Can we go now?" Dark and terrible thoughts swirled in the back of his mind right now, not the happy, relaxed place he normally inhabited. This was closer to the bad old days before the Academy. Javier thought he had put all that behind him.

Sykora watched him for a second longer, alpha dog making a point, before she stepped back and moved to one side. "Let's go, Yu."

Javier followed the man out of engineering and up a deck to D. They both staggered like drunks, holding onto the handrail lest they slide all the way back down the sharp staircase.

Sykora led Javier back to his cell and shoved him in. She disconnected the manacles, and flipped an energy bar, the kind that tasted like sawdust and raw sewage, onto the bed before activating the force field.

Javier was just happy that the field was in place. It would keep him from doing anything terminally stupid at this moment. Not that he didn't consider it. "How about a shower?" he asked, just loud enough to be heard.

She smiled, a content little giant princess in her castle. "There's a sink," she said. "The bed has a blanket." And she was gone.

Javier sat on the center of the bed. That wench was seriously messing with his *wa*. He folded up his legs and began to meditate.

He had bathed in the sink and then cat-napped and meditated for several hours. Homicidal tendencies had been pushed well to the back of his mind.

For now.

Not forgotten.

He wasn't that person, any more. They wouldn't make him go back there. Not today.

Escape was primary. Vengeance could come later. But first he had to survive.

A knock at the doorway brought him to the surface. "Javier?" It was Machinist's Mate Yu.

Javier cracked an eye, saw a shadow outside the force field. The cell was dim enough that he was almost invisible on the bed. He started flexing muscles to loosen everything up without visible motion. Sykora was not to be seen.

"Javier," Yu called again, louder. "Time to wake up. Captain wants to see you."

That got the eyes open. For the briefest moment, Javier considered overpowering the slim man and making a break for it, but there was nowhere to go. He was a week's sail to get to anyplace civilized from here, and no boat. Survival first. Still, it was Yu and not Sykora. Silver linings.

Javier climbed off the bed slowly. "Yeah, Ilan," he called, "I'm coming." He stretched everything as he approached the force field. He sighed, mostly due to lack of tea to kick-start his morning. That and freshly-pulled honey made things much nicer in deep space.

Yu shut off the force field with a smile. "Ready?"

Javier looked at him sidelong for a moment. "No manacles?" he asked.

Yu grinned and shook his head. "Captain said to ask real nice and you'd probably behave," he said simply.

Javier felt a chill at the bottom of his stomach. Pirates didn't act like this, not even the romantic ones in the movies. They were cut-throat professional businessmen.

They wanted something.

Javier followed Yu to the Captain's office and watched him knock. The door slid sideways on silent pneumatics. Javier followed Yu into the room.

Captain Sokolov was at his desk, like before. He looked exactly like a ship's captain was supposed to, according to all the movies. He still had that charisma-thing captains were supposed to have. Javier had never gotten the hang of it. It probably helped to actually like people.

Sykora had apparently decided to get dressed up this morning. She was wearing a *Neu Berne* Field Combat Uniform. Considering her size and mass, it was probably custom tailored. Certainly freshly pressed. It came with a pistol and a short saber. Probably for effect. Probably.

Nobody else was in the room.

Captain Sokolov smiled warmly at Javier and gestured to the seat. "Please, Javier," he said amiably, "have a seat. Yu, don't go far. I'll want to talk to you after this."

Yu did something that approximated a salute in some cultures and skedaddled.

Javier took a long moment to size up Sykora. Not that he intended to do anything stupid. Here, anyway. Mostly just to remind himself not to be intimidated by the giantess with the quick fists. He sat and eyed Captain Sokolov closely. "Captain."

A long moment passed as the two men judged each other.

Sokolov took a drink from his steaming mug. "I woke up this morning," he began, "and my head felt better." He sipped and watched Javier for a response.

Javier blinked once.

The Captain plowed on. "I wanted to say thank you."

Javier nodded. Still not willing to commit. Something about lack of a shower and hot meal and morning tea and still horribly smelly air caused his manners to be atrocious this morning.

Sokolov seemed to understand. "So now I have a conundrum."

Javier resisted speaking some more. Sykora in dress uniform might mean she wanted to make nice, and it might be appropriate for an execution. *Neu Berne* troopers tended to be sticklers for details. He glanced up at her, lingered, returned. She scowled professionally back.

"I spoke with Dragoon Sykora," Sokolov continued, "and she tells me you handled the bio-scrubber rebuild very professionally, including showing Yu how to fabricate a bypass for a burned out number six lead."

Curiosity got the better of him. "Why can't your

Engineer keep those systems running?" Javier asked in the pause.

He was rewarded with Sokolov's awkward glance at Sykora and a deep breath to compose his thoughts. "Dalca is a mid-functioning introvert," he said, pausing to think.

Javier cocked his head. "So are lots of engineers," he replied. "That's why they become engineers in the first place."

Sokolov nodded. "Correct," he said, "and she's quite good. However…"

Javier waited.

"Apparently," Sokolov continued, "the bio-scrubber *bit* her."

"Bit her?" Javier repeated. Understanding dawned. "Ah. So now she won't touch it."

Javier had never gotten anyone to explain it to him better than that. Something bad had happened to them with a particular piece of machinery, it had *bit* them, and they would develop what was, to an extrovert like him, a total neurosis. Introverts made great engineers, most of the time. This was the drawback.

Sokolov nodded sagely. "Exactly. I can't exactly requisition new Machinist's Mates out here, and she can't train people."

Javier smiled evilly. "Good luck then, Captain."

"Which brings me," Sokolov said, "to you."

Javier felt a chill go up his spine. He felt Sykora's smile without looking over.

Javier blinked.

Sokolov at least had the decency to look pained at the words coming out of his mouth. "Normally," he began, "I would sell you off as inmate labor on one of the mining colonies we work with occasionally." A pause to sip at his coffee, reading Javier's face. "In your case, maybe one of the farming worlds where your expertise with plants and animals might be handy."

A long pause. Javier refused to rise to the bait. He wasn't about to let the Captain off his own hook.

"Depending on circumstances and timing," Sokolov finally continued in the silence, "you would be worth twenty-five hundred to three thousand credits to me from such a transaction. I would like to talk to you about honor."

Javier almost snorted out loud. Or sputtered. Hard to tell. Certainly, this was the moment in the movies where someone did a spit-take all over someone else. He drew a breath, careful about how close to the edge he probably was right now. "A pirate, talking honor?"

Sokolov got a very hard look on his face. Captain's Face. "I'm talking about two Academy men under awkward circumstances. And it's not about my honor. It's about yours."

Javier leaned back in his chair, suddenly aware how far forward he had been leaning. A slap might have been less surprising. Well, maybe not, considering Sykora's penchant for mild physical violence. "Mine. Mine?"

"Yours," Sokolov pronounced. "I would like to offer you a deal."

Javier would have liked to have not gotten out of bed this morning. Nothing that had happened had improved that notion. "A deal?"

Sokolov waited for more. None was forthcoming.

"My crew," the Captain began, "are paid reasonable wages. For a ship that wanders on both sides of legality, we do well. I would like to offer you a contract of indenture against your honor. Your ransom, if you will, as an officer and a gentleman. I will value you at twenty-five hundred credits. As a First-Rate-Spacer, you could pay off that debt in seven years as a member of this crew, and then would be free to go."

Javier resisted goggling. Barely. Definitely not what he had planned when he got up this morning. He remembered to breathe. And decided to push his luck. It was what he did best, anyway. Just ask his ex-wives. "What about your Centurions? What do they make?"

Sokolov blinked, slightly taken aback. "My Centurions," he nodded to Sykora as an example, "profit-share." Javier watched him juggle numbers in his head. "In your case, roughly four years, less if we had a big score."

Javier leaned well back into the chair and thought. Lose, lose, and lose. Be a corpse, be a slave, be a pirate. At least pirates dressed well. Maybe he could ask for a fancy sash. You never knew when you'd need a fancy sash. And, worse come to worst, he could sabotage the ship and blow the whole thing to hell if they pushed him far enough. Make the universe a better place.

Javier leaned forward, mentally flipped a coin. Rosencrantz and Guildenstern would be proud. "I have met your Dragoon and your Engineer," he began. "I presume you have a Gunner, a Boatswain, and a Purser. And the medbay is automated enough that you don't need a Surgeon. You could hire me as your *Science Officer.*" *Heads.*

He watched Sokolov do mental gymnastics. The man did sputter, but he wasn't used to dealing with Javier. He would learn. Or not.

Javier waited.

"Why in the world," the Captain finally said, "would a pirate vessel need a Science Officer?"

Javier smiled. "Why, indeed?"

Captain Zakhar Sokolov, Commanding Officer of the private-service Strike Corvette *Storm Gauntlet*, *Concord* Fleet career veteran, and pirate extraordinaire, looked down into his mug of coffee as if he could read the future on the dregs contained therein. Apparently, he had hired himself a Science Officer.

And it had been Aritza.

He wasn't sure if that was the smartest thing he had ever done, or the dumbest.

Certainly, a free-lance vessel like his needed every edge he could give it. Would this sarcastic fast-talker be a boon or a bramble? Only time would tell.

He took a deep breath as Sykora returned from escorting Aritza into the hall. The hatch whispered closed.

They held eyes for a few moments, before she shrugged and looked down.

"Yu," he said into the long quiet, "is not sneaky enough to keep a close watch on that man, so I'll settle for regular reports from the rest of the crew."

Djamila Sykora, Dragoon of the pirate vessel *Storm Gauntlet*, combat veteran of ground, sea, and space; giantess; and recreational knitter, came to parade rest just inside the closed door. "I can get close to him," she replied, perhaps a touch defensive.

Zakhar cocked his head. "Djamila," he began, "the first time you met, you shot him. The second time, according to the reports, you beat him up and gave him a concussion. Then you worked him for seven hours fixing the bio-scrubber before throwing him back into the brig." He grinned a little as he paused to take a sip. "If he were a horse, we'd call that riding him hard and putting him away wet. Plus, I've seen the gleam he gets in his eye when he looks at you."

He watched her square her massive shoulders up a little tighter. "I can take him," she said.

"Djamila," the Captain replied, "he's not going to warn you it's coming."

She thought about it and smiled brittlely. "So what do we do?"

Sokolov considered his options. "You and the crew treat him like any other Centurion. And keep a close tab. I didn't promise not to kill him."

He watched her salute, pivot, and exit with all the professionalism he had come to expect from her.

He had a good crew. Would it be enough?

BOOK TWO: SHIPWRECK

Javier stood in the pirate ship's cavernous cargo bay and considered the possibilities. Torpedoes were big, expensive, and hard to acquire in private practice. Sokolov had reduced the eighty launch silos on E and F decks to twelve tubes forward, six on each side. Only seven were actually loaded.

The remaining space had been opened up for cargo storage, spanned by the original trestles and frames, plus a small flight deck containing a battered transport tug that had started life in the *Daxing* Navy a century ago as an assault shuttle.

Sokolov had been true to his threats. *Mielikki* had been cut into sections and parted out. She had been too customized and automated to reprogram in less than a year and a half anyway, even if they did have someone on crew to do it. Javier certainly wasn't about to help. Whole frames of the little vessel had been cut away to get to the engines, sensors, and jump drives, so they could be unceremoniously pulled aboard *Storm Gauntlet* and stored.

Somehow, however, Javier had convinced the pirates to

protect the cargo sections of *Mielikki* containing the arboretum and botany station. It had been wrapped up, insulated, cut out like a plum's stone from *Mielikki's* carcass, and brought onto the flight deck. Sokolov had even turned off all the gravity plates in the rear half of the corvette so the crew could slide it forward into the foremost port cargo space and link it in to ship's power and the water system. In a couple of weeks, after some more tuning of the life support generators and the bio-scrubbers, he might even connect the hydroponics section externally and let his fish clean the ship's water.

Let them drink fish poop. It would still be an improvement.

Javier keyed the security lock and stepped into his sanctum. Provisional Machinist's Mate Ilan Yu, now his aide, bodyguard, and minder, was close behind.

Inside, Yu grabbed his elbow suddenly. "Are those real cherries?" he asked, wonder in his voice.

Javier smiled as he pulled the primary bin of chicken feed from the shelf. "They are," he replied.

"What are you going to do with them?"

The reality of the situation hit. Javier scowled and shrugged. "When it was just me," he said, "I'd have eaten half and made cherry wine with the rest." When he didn't have any master but boredom. And chickens.

"Really?" Yu asked. "Cherry wine? That's a thing?"

Javier sighed, quietly, mostly to himself. People, again. It was almost as bad as his Fleet days. "It's like this, Ilan. Fresh fruit lasts for days. Dried fruit lasts for weeks. Canned fruit lasts for months. But fermented fruit will last for years."

The tall, skinny, Asian guy lit up. "Really? That's cool. So can we make some?"

Javier shook his head. "Afraid not," he said. "These

sixteen little gems are going to the Officer's Wardroom as a treat. Make that fifteen. This one looks bad." Javier picked a red and gold orb the size of a large marble from a branch and inspected its perfection.

He handed it to Yu. "You should eat this one and make sure it hasn't been ruined or something." He had a mock-serious smile on this face.

Yu took the cherry from him with reverence due a priceless religious artifact. "Wow. Thanks."

Javier had his first smile of the day. Or maybe the week. Hard to tell. "Bite slowly, Ilan," he said. "It has a pit in the middle, a little stone. It can damage your teeth, and your teeth can damage the seed. I want to keep it, plant it and grow more."

Yu ate his first ever Rainier cherry with a look of pure ecstasy.

While Yu was distracted, Javier cracked open the bin of chicken feed and rooted around until he found the chip containing Suvi. Good, she was still safe. Nowhere to go, now that her ship had been dismembered, but at least she had survived. He pushed her to the bottom of the bin and pulled out the measuring cup, filled with seeds and vitamins.

In the next space, they found four emotionally-damaged chickens rooting hungrily in the vegetable patch. The first toss of grain brought them all close, angrily scolding him, and each other, and the grass, and everything else.

They were chickens.

JAVIER WATCHED Yu sit down across the table from him and slide his lunch tray into the locks to keep it in place. He felt talked out, after three hours.

Yu was irrepressible. "So, Javier," he paused, an embarrassed look on his face. "Wait, I'm supposed to call you Mr. Aritza in public. You're a Centurion, now."

Javier sighed. This was why he was a civilian now. Stupid, petty rules. "Ilan, call me whatever you want. I'm pretty sure Sykora will slip up and call me shit-head at some point. I'll probably answer."

Yu shrugged. "Captain runs a tight ship," he said.

That kind of ended the conversation. Javier called it a tie and went back to his extruded protein sludge that the mess computer called pudding. His recipe was better, but he used real beets for sugar, instead of cracked industrial chemicals. In about twelve days, he'd have a batch of golden beets ready for harvest. Then he'd show them.

Across the way, he watched another crewmember add his name to the lottery drawing. Every day, the computer randomly selected a crewman from the list to have fresh eggs for breakfast. It messed up Javier's morning routine, but what he was eating was close enough to fleet food, and it would make the crew much more well-disposed towards the new officer.

"So, Ilan," Javier scraped the bottom of the bowl with his spoon. Not bad. Not as good as he could do, but about normal for a fleet vessel, which was pretty good for a pirate. "What's on your mind?"

Javier watched the ground between then start to open.

"Well, sir," Yu said, now a crewman addressing a Centurion instead of two guys having lunch, "what's a Science Officer actually do?" He sipped from a bulb of something. "I mean, besides raise chickens and vegetables and stuff."

Javier thought about it for a moment. Two weeks had already passed. He was already falling back into Fleet routines.

Yuck.

"Today," he said, "I'm going to calibrate the new sensor array they stripped off of my ship, off *Mielikki*. Engineering and Damage Control finally got everything wired two shifts ago." Javier drank some *tea*, wincing at the taste. "Eventually, they'll strip out your old ones and free up hull space."

Yu was entranced. "Are they that much better than ours?"

Javier considered the launch dates of *Storm Gauntlet* and *Mielikki*. "Yu," he smiled to take the sting out of the words. "*Mielikki* was a probe-cutter outfitted for survey work. My survey pod is probably six or eight times more powerful than yours. *Storm Gauntlet* is a warship. Shoot things and move on. I'm used to sitting on the edge of a system for two or three days, plotting the moons orbits for planets on the far side of a sun, before I jump closer." He took another drink. "Much better."

Yu nodded to himself and dug into his food. "Sounds good, sir," he said between bites. "Let me finish this and I'll escort you to the bridge."

Javier was careful not to let the scowl reach his face. Yu was doing his job. All that squank about honor and ransom didn't stop the Captain from assigning him a minder and escort, everywhere he went.

Could be worse, though. At least Sykora had kept her distance.

***

JAVIER KNEW BETTER than to ascribe it to luck. Even bad luck.

Just as he settled into his new workstation on the bridge, Sykora entered and moved to a space facing him from across the bridge. She was wearing a pistol this morning. Unusual.

And had a nice clean field of fire at him if she wanted. Not unusual.

Javier decided not to say anything to Yu. She was probably a good enough shot that there wouldn't be any collateral damage if things got out of hand. Not that he was planning to do anything stupid today. Not here.

He watched the Machinist's Mate settle in to the workstation facing his, mirroring Javier's display so he could watch and learn.

Javier decided to find the silver lining and pulled out the headphones. He handed them to Yu as he pushed a few buttons to change Yu's display to a training mode, with his own screen in a corner.

Yu got a panicked look on his face. "What happened?" he whispered.

Javier grinned. "Put them on," he said, "and start working your way through the training simulations." He settled into his chair and toggled through options. "I'm going to be calibrating for the next three hours, and eventually you need to know how all this stuff works, if you're going to keep being my sidekick."

Yu relaxed, strapped himself in, and went to work with the sort of single-mindedness he had shown in the bio-scrubber. Not much imagination, but lots of enthusiasm. Javier had had worse yeoman working for him, back in the day. He looked over as the Captain emerged from his day cabin and relieved the Gunner from the watch.

Sokolov speared him across the bridge with all the seriousness one could put into being The Captain.

"Mr. Aritza," he said, Commanding Officer addressing a junior Centurion on a new deck. "Are we ready to proceed?"

Javier had to resist the urge to salute or something. Too much of Fleet was coming back to the surface. He didn't want to be that guy any more. A glance at Sykora. Or lunch for the black widow in the corner. "Affirmative, Captain," he said, crisply. "Give the word."

Sokolov nodded. "What are our specifications, Mister?"

Javier decided to play along. The Captain was making a show for the rest of the bridge crew, people who were strangers to Javier for the most part, unprepared for a sudden eruption of caustic sarcasm in their midst. "Well, sir," he replied. "How well does *Storm Gauntlet* compare to the old *Bannockburn*?"

Javier watched a small grin cross the Captain's mouth for a second. Only two Academy grads could have that conversation. It set a good tone, considering the rest were likely outcasts and dregs of various navies, put to shore by drink, temperament, or budget cuts. "Without a dedicated Science Officer," the captain announced, "she's probably comparable to the Academy Training Corvette. Perhaps five to ten percent better at shorter ranges. Less so at distance."

So, about what Javier expected for a boat like this. The sensor pods were cheap and durable, and probably older than about half the crew. "In that case, Captain, I would expect to improve on that by a factor of four or five after initial calibration, and six afterwards. If I had access to the kind of tuned automation that had been written for my old probe-cutter, as much as ten."

Javier could hear the gasps and snorts around them, depending on whether or not people believed him or thought he was boasting. He gave the whole bridge crew a carnivorous smile, lingering for a special moment on Sykora. She could have been carved from white marble.

He turned to the Navigator, a big Dutchman who seemed to know what he was about. "If you'd like to watch, we could bring up screen fourteen on the main display." The man nodded at him. "Fifty percent transparency, please. Thirty percent overlay."

The big screen in front of the captain split into two images, almost identical, with the old pod readings on the left and the pod from *Mielikki*, brought up to *Storm Gauntlet's* calibration, on the right.

Javier approved. The man was decisive and professional. Sokolov seemed able to surround himself with good people. Getting them all hung from the highest yardarm would probably make him feel bad. Afterwards. For a little while.

"Captain," he followed up, "permission to hard ping the system to baseline my systems?"

Sokolov played along nicely. "Approved."

Javier unlocked a control on his touch screen with a password, and pressed the revealed button. Like every other default sensor control system in space, it emitted a sound like an old wet-navy sonar system pinging. He smiled. Some engineer, centuries ago, had achieved a personal form of immortality.

He paused and watched his local screen, overlain with a mask as he supervised Yu's training. There shouldn't be anything hard enough to generate a return wave for several light minutes in any direction. This was the boring part he always left for Suvi.

After several minutes, he opened up the configuration console and began tinkering. The system had about eleven hours of passive data to work with. He started adjusting things to the sorts of baseline values he already knew from years with this hardware, as if everything was new. No point in letting them know what he could really do.

A little red diamond appeared on his screen as the computer started washing noise out of the signal. Sokolov was apparently paying closer attention that he let on. He leaned forward. "Mr. Aritza?" was all he said.

Javier was already dialing the signal in and decoding the information. "Stand by," he said.

That can't be right.

Can it?

Huh.

"Captain," Javier said into the pregnant silence. "that appears to be a very old emergency beacon on the fourth planet, which appears to be habitable." Leave it at that. He really needed more information to draw better conclusions. Better to be kind of ignorant at this point and show off later.

Sokolov tore his eyes from the screen to look over. "How old, Mister?"

Javier could read the avarice in his voice.

Avarice? Right, pirates. All about money.

"Sir," he said. Damn, this was just like the Fleet days. Maybe he needed to paint his monitor lavender or something. Just to keep him from getting all serious and stuff. "If the crash date being broadcast is correct, at least seventeen years." But. "However, the power source is extremely weak, and well past its expected lifespan." And the kicker. "You would normally have had to be almost in orbit in order to pick it up, if you weren't looking." Or hadn't just hired an expert on sensor systems to go beyond standard baselines.

Sokolov was doing calculations in his head. "That suggests survivors maintaining it, or at least good maintenance worksystem robots," he said. He turned to the Navigator. "Mr. Alferdinck, plot a jump to get us close. Ms. Sykora, prepare a landing team and wake Smith up to fly you in." He saved the best for last. "Mr. Aritza, you will accompany Sykora's team to investigate the wreck."

Javier goggled at him, completely off-guard. "What do I know about xeno-archaeology?"

Sokolov got that evil Captain's smile going. "The fact that you even know the word puts you ahead of most of the crew, Javier. That's why I hired a Science Officer."

Javier cursed inside as he unbuckled from his seat. That man was entirely too good at this.

On one hand, things wouldn't be boring.

On the other hand, surviving these people long enough to have them all arrested was going to be a task.

Crap.

PART TWO

Javier grabbed Yu and swung by the cargo deck for a quick teaching session.

"Okay, Ilan," he said, "since I'm going to be down on the planet for however long, you're in charge of feeding the chickens. First step, locate them. I'll wait here."

Yu goggled at him briefly, then put on his serious face and headed aft.

Javier let go a breath and grabbed the feed bin. He set it on the counter, cracked it open, and thrust a hand in.

There. Suvi.

He closed his fist and pulled his best friend out, sliding her into a pocket, safe. If they had found her, his life wouldn't be worth a bucket of warm spit.

Yu clomped back into the botany station. "Found them," he beamed. "Sleeping in the apple trees."

"Good," Javier replied. He pointed at the feed bucket. "That's chicken feed. Don't worry about refilling the bucket today. I have more in cold storage." He picked it up and handed it into Yu's uncomprehending clutches.

Ilan looked kinda lost, which was the point here.

"What next?" he said softly.

Javier smiled. "Now you open it up, fill the scoop halfway, close the bucket, and follow me into the forward bay where the fruit bushes are."

He paused as Yu di so, the image of serious scholarship. They headed forward.

Surrounded by fruit bushes and meta-dwarf and columnar fruit trees, Javier gave Yu a serious look. "Okay. Now cluck."

"I beg your pardon?" Yu's face went completely slack.

"Cluck," Javier said. "Like this." He made a sound with his teeth and tongue.

Yu repeated the sound, sort of. A few times.

"Good," Javier said. "Athos will usually find you first. d'Artagnan will almost always be last. Just stand here clucking until all four arrive, and scatter a little grain as you see each one."

Javier stepped back as the first hungry lady arrived in a fluster of wings.

Yu dumped a little of the grain out, and was suddenly ankle deep in chickens as two more surrounded him.

"Good, Ilan," Javier beamed. "Do this every morning around the start of day shift. And make sure you check their water dish in the vegetable garden. You'll probably need to fill it every three days or so."

"What about you?" Yu asked, a little panicked.

"I'm going to be planet-side, probably for a couple of days at least. Enjoy."

Javier stepped out of the room, down the hall, and out of the arboretum.

Suvi was safe, for now. Now he just had to avoid getting killed by crazy dragon-lady.

AFT, on the flight deck, Javier decided he really liked the assault shuttle pilot. Delridge Smith was a gray-haired lunatic who favored Hawaiian print shirts and talked a mile a minute.

The tiny flight deck of the assault shuttle, separated from the aft section by a seriously sturdy airlock, was decorated like a Merankorr brothel, all pinks and pastels, with Terran Caribbean music playing quietly in the background. Javier watched as the man completed a very detailed and thorough pre-flight check, literally touching everything as he went, talking to himself under his breath the whole time.

Javier felt safer just watching.

He felt Sykora arrive.

He still felt safe. Maybe.

She was wearing field gear: light on armor and long on camouflage patterns that slowly moved as he stared. It kinda looked like bread baking, the slow bubbling effect as dots and stripes evolved. He wasn't sure if it was going to make him motion sick if he stared long enough.

Sykora was armed to the teeth, with a knife, a pistol on her hip, another knife, a second pistol in a shoulder rig, and a big, nasty battlerifle slung on her back. He had known street gangs less well armed. Of course, most of them were also less dangerous than this woman.

She was also carrying a familiar-looking backpack. His. She walked up and handed it to him with a simple "Here."

Javier flipped it open and looked inside. Everything was generally in place. He smiled up at her. "Thanks for repacking it cleanly. I told you the only firearm I owned was the pistol in my cabin."

She shrugged. "It was still necessary to confirm." Her eyes conveyed a certain level of distaste, but that might be for someone who didn't own enough weapons to impress her.

He decided to ask, anyway. "Any chance I could get it

back, since we're going down onto the surface of a potentially hostile planet?" He even tried to sound charming.

She smiled at him in the way grown-ups do with rambunctious eight-year-olds. "You'll have me," she said serenely. "I'll protect you from the bad men."

Javier was pretty sure Gandhi would have lacked the willpower not to roll his eyes at that one. He wasn't Gandhi, so he did. And then pulled out his sensor remote and toggled the settings to confirm everything was ready to go.

She leaned over his shoulder to look. "What is that?" she said, at least trying to sound nice.

He glanced sidelong, and up, at her, close enough to kiss, or bite. Decisions, decisions. "Short-range airborne autonomous remote," he said as he pulled it out of the pack. It looked like a knobby, gray, grapefruit.

Javier flipped the power on and gave it a soft toss into the air, like a beach ball. It hovered about a meter over his head, rotated a few times as it mapped the flight deck, and began a slow orbit of the space.

Javier pulled the matching portable computer from the bag and powered up the relay controls. The room was mapped in visual, ultrasound, radar, and infrared, with a stack of dials and gauges giving him various readings on people and equipment.

Sykora eyed it professionally. "Is that thing armed?" Of course. Trust the killer to go *there* immediately. Still, a two-meter-tall wall of professional paranoia between him and bad things planetside wasn't necessarily the worst idea he'd had today.

"Not this model," Javier pushed the recall and watched it settle lightly into his open palm. "I rarely set down on a planet without scanning it hard to begin with, so I know where the dangerous carnivores are, usually. This is mostly for working in tight quarters, like cave systems."

She was still an expert. "Or wrecked starships," she said, already adjusting her tactical planning. Scary. Good, but scary.

The pilot rescued him from any further comments as he wandered over. "Any time you're ready, Sykora," he said. "Gonna man the turret going down?"

She shook her head. "This isn't a hot LZ, Del," she replied, counting crew members to make sure everyone was there. "I'll ride with the rest in back."

"Suit yourself," he said. He turned and walked up the big rear landing deck and into the small airlock. As Javier watched, the man grinned at him, waved, and cycled the hatch closed.

Sykora completed her own count and looked around. "Mount up, people," she called, walking up the ramp.

Javier watched around a half dozen people file into the shuttle ahead of him. Two were obviously security goons, armed and armored up like their boss. Two females that looked like scouts. A couple of regular crew he recognized vaguely from Engineering.

Inside, he found Sykora in a jump seat at the top of the ramp. She patted the one next to her. "Aritza," she said, command voice invoked, "you sit here." One seat was as good as the next, so Javier settled and strapped himself in while she watched. She nodded when he was done, apparently satisfied that he wasn't a total landsman. Little did she know.

Sykora pulled on a field helmet and keyed a microphone live. "Gunship One, we are go for launch."

A red light came on, flashing, followed by a horn hooting, and then the ramp began to rise, closing with the solemnity of a bank vault. Interior lighting came up at the same time and the shuttle began to vibrate and hum as the pilot brought systems on line.

A nudge in his ribs, just as he closed his eyes, leaned back, and prepared to nap. "You're going to sleep through this?" Sykora looked shocked.

Javier shrugged, at least as much as he could in five-point harness. "Not my first time in an assault shuttle, lady," he said over the growing racket. "We're probably fifteen minutes to clear the ship from here, forty minutes orbital to match ground windows, and then an hour to get low enough to deploy the wings. Another hour to scout a landing spot and settle."

She scowled professionally at him. "We need to go over the plan for when we land."

Javier looked at her with a lazy smile. "I'm the scientist, you're the big, dumb, gun bunny. I scan the wreck. You shoot things. Not hard at all." He closed his eyes and leaned back.

She poked him harder this time. "That's what you think of me?" she asked. There was a new edge to her voice. "Just another killer?"

Javier couldn't resist. He already owed her. Several times over, if he thought about it. He opened his eyes, let them roam over her whole body, lingering in the girlie places, before he made eye contact. "Yes." And then he closed them again and tuned her out.

PART THREE

SYKORA SETTLED into her drop station, secured in place as the last fuel connection severed with a ping that rattled hollowly through the shuttle.

Djamila seethed.

Like all things, it was internal. In *Neu Berne* society, image and social station were everything. She had learned that early, the daughter of a manual laborer and a former "entertainer." The Navy had promised her an open society, where one could advance based purely on merit and skill. And it had been, but only to a point. She had had to prove herself better than everyone, man and woman, to be accepted.

But she had. Oh, yes, she had. First in her training crèche. Record scores on physical fitness, obstacle course, and survival training. Elite tactical school. Zero-G combat school, where she had earned the nickname "Ballerina of Death" for her ability to move in powered armor in three dimensions, with a weapon in each hand.

She had been the best.

It had even been good enough for a poor, blue-collar

waif, with no family connections and no university, to be commissioned as an Officer and a Frieholder. But it could not get her accepted. Not by the elite of the *Neu Berne* Navy.

Not *them.*

They were the scions of generations of service, intermarried almost to incestuous degrees. Money. Power. Connections. The right boarding schools. The right summer vacations at the same wealthy enclaves and terra-formed moons. She could still see their sneers as they *welcomed* her, the poor girl who had risen so far above her station. So far.

She was never accepted. Never one of *them.* She remembered her last commanding officer explaining that she was good enough to promote, but lacked the interest of powerful players to advance her career. She was dead-ended. It was enough to drive her to resign and strike out into deep space, where people like that didn't control her destiny.

And now, sitting right next to her, looking down his nose at her, another one of *them.* Another educated elite prick, from the *Concord* Academy on *Bryce*, no less, who thought she was just a well-trained bulldog bitch.

Captain Sokolov was the only superior who had ever looked at her as a person. He had rescued her from falling into the pit itself when she lost her way, given her a place again, a purpose, a job. He was the Captain.

So Djamila seethed. She considered just smashing Aritza into the bulkhead, like last time. It would be rewarding to pound on him.

But wouldn't that lend credence to his belief that she was just *another dumb gun bunny?* Wouldn't that prove *them* right about her? Excellent for kicking in doors, but not someone you invite to a cocktail party? A well-trained bulldog bitch?

She wouldn't let them win.

Her jaw hurt from grinding her teeth.

Djamila blinked, surprised at the sudden swell of

emotions that flowed over her. Normally, she was calmness itself. This runt just somehow pushed all her buttons.

She would have to work on that. And prove them, *him*, wrong.

She smiled hard. Very wrong.

THE RIDE down was smoother than Javier had ever experienced in any assault shuttle. It was more like riding in a VIP transport with an Admiral.

He really liked this pilot.

And the crazy ogre lady had left him alone for the whole trip.

He had been half-expecting more grief from her. Lord knew, he was dancing right up on the edge of rude. It was like poking a sleeping bear, or a missing tooth. Irresistible.

And she had a short fuse. But those military types, all structure and order and pattern, really grated on him. He just couldn't resist. Chickens were still better company.

More than once, Javier had opened his eyes to glance over at the Dragoon, wondering if she had fallen asleep. But the eyes had been open, just lost deep in thought. Probably planning firing lanes and organizing watch shifts. Something very military.

Outside, the whistle of air over the hull was augmented by a soft thump as the wings began to deploy, softly biting into the thickening air. Javier yawned and stretched. He really liked this pilot.

LEMUEL LOOKED up in mild surprise at the sound of

thunder. The day had dawned clear and cool, with a nice autumn breeze. There should be no rain.

A glint of light in the northern sky. Movement. It took his brain several more seconds to process the image as the giant, gray-black bird resolved itself into an aircraft approaching, orbiting twice, and then flying east to the grassy plain where the herdbeasts calved in the spring.

It had been years since technology.

A stray though flitted across his mind. *Others* were coming. *Strangers* come to violate his virgin wilderness. He would have to welcome *them* properly. He walked a few steps down the hill to where Anya, Mohr, and Thomas were buried. They had not lasted long enough to see this day.

Lemuel glanced back at the wreckage he had called home for so long, smiled, and strode down the path to the river.

Welcome *them* **properly**.

JAVIER WATCHED Sykora move with an economy of grace. For a woman who was all knees and elbows and shoulders, there was not a wasted motion or a foot put wrong. He still didn't like her, but he could respect pure professionalism when it bit him on the ass.

As long as she didn't actually bite him on the ass.

He smiled to himself and stayed out of her way as he tossed the sensor remote into the air and let it baseline the area around the shuttle.

The air had a strange smell, but every new planet did. It's what happened when you got away from industrial air-processors and let plants and oceans clean things. It was also cool, a sunny day low on the horizon, so either spring or fall, depending.

Javier dialed down the sensitivity on the remote and

pushed the scan range out as far as it would go. The original wreck was about six kilometers northeast, tucked up in a small valley drained by a creek. In another twenty minutes, he would have a very detailed map about halfway out. The rest would have to wait until they got around some hills for direct scanning.

There were quite a few creatures nearby, four-legged animals that seemed to be the local version of elk or antelope. Javier turned and located Sykora in the organized mess of landing. Once more, just because. "Hey," he called, "any chance I can have a sidearm for protection?"

The look he got in return could have smashed a glacier. Javier suddenly understood the term 'staring daggers.' "You've got me," was all she said in reply.

Well, then. All-righty. Javier opened his field pack and put on a floppy hat.

Javier found a landing skid that was cool enough and plopped down. He pulled a screwdriver from his kit and opened the side of the portable. When nobody was paying attention, he palmed the chip that had Suvi on it and plugged her into the side of the little computer. It was going to be a tiny shoebox compared to the castle she was used to living in, but it was something. And he could use somebody to talk to right now that he didn't want to see hung from the highest yardarm in space.

Javier muted the speakers and waited. She didn't take long.

Where am I?

Javier typed quickly on the rudimentary keyboard. This was not a conversation to have while surrounded by the bad guys listening in.

Pirates caught us. Trashed the ship. I hid you. You're plugged into the sensor drone's command portable. They don't know about you. Keep it that way. JA

He couldn't imagine she liked the idea, but there wasn't much she could do.

Where are we?

Campeche 7, still. Wrecked starship nearby they want to loot. We have to help.

They're pirates!!!

And we're not dead. Survival first. Vengeance later. Promise.

<pout />

Javier figured it was a draw. Hopefully, Suvi would listen for a while and understand where they were. Having her available just doubled his chances.

And now, the mucking in the mud part.

Unlike all the hard-edged military sophistication around him, his gear was, beyond the sensor remote, decidedly low-tech, almost stupidly so. A magnetic compass. Matches. Pencil and paper for hand-made maps and notes. He did have a small knife, but it was made from a steel alloy and sharpened on a stone. It didn't even vibrate or have a laser-cutting edge, or a mono-molecular razor-sharp blade. Just a knife.

Javier pulled out a nifty little plastic hiking trinket he had picked up years ago. It had a very cheap magnetic compass, a thermometer, and the symbols you should make in the dirt in an emergency, for people searching for you. He clipped it onto the outside of his jacket and marveled. Way better impulse buy at a feed supply store than any candy bar had ever been.

Around him, Sykora's troopers prepared to invade Guatemala.

Javier sat quietly, daydreaming until a tree suddenly cast a shadow over him.

"Are we boring you, Aritza?"

Javier looked up at the ogress, scowling down at him. Maybe honey today, instead of vinegar? What the hell. "No ma'am," he said with a grin, "trying to stay out of your way while your crew organized itself. We ready?"

He was rewarded by the scowl lessening, warming by perhaps a whole degree Kelvin. Nitrogen might melt soon at this rate.

She stepped back, rather than lurk over him. "What's the terrain look like?" she asked, apparently also striving for courtesy. Maybe there was hope.

Javier flipped on the portable's hologram projector. A color-coded terrain map hovered between them, green for trees, brown for grass, gray for rock. Southwest, it just kept gently rolling to a distant sea. Northeast, their goal, the details slowly filled in.

Javier checked a readout to one side. Exactly one transmission source other than the shuttle, anywhere within range. And even here on the surface it was weak. He pushed the remote up another two hundred meters, until it was barely a dot in the clear sky above them. Nothing was going to be shooting at it, fingers crossed.

The wreck suddenly appeared bright on the radar, refined metals covered with dirt amidst scrub on the edge of a forest. It looked like the ship was a small freighter, maybe seventy or one hundred meters long. From the debris field, she had come in pretty hot, plowed through a bunch of trees, barely under control, and broken her back when she slammed down, with three major sections of hull mostly intact, and shards over a fairly compact area.

He glanced back up, but Sykora was intent on the display, not him. She really had nice teeth.

"Any radiation leakage from the wreck?" she asked. And always business.

Javier felt his shoulders shrug. "No more than normal background," he said. "Looks like it landed soft enough to protect the reactors. No load now except the emergency beacon, and it's faint, so they're fading. Maybe another year before they go."

He saw the ghost of a smile actually cross her face for the first time today. "So," she looked down at him, all business again, "something worth salvaging, after all."

"Looks like," he said, unwilling to commit more from the scans. He really didn't know what this ship, this crew did when they weren't all piratey. Maybe they funded orphanages. Space was big. There were a lot of weird people out there.

Javier watched Sykora go full tactical before his eyes. It was like a switch flipped on.

"Base team," she called, a parade ground voice that echoed off the trees, "establish a perimeter. Smith, unlock the guns but don't shoot first." A group of spacers looked up from their tasks and variously kept in motion.

One of the gun bunnies even saluted. "On it, ma'am," he said, all crisp and professional. And ready for Thermopylae.

She pointed in the direction of the wreck. "Pathfinders, north-east and stay sharp. Hostile planet." Two women nodded and faded into the brush, vanishing as he watched. They seemed more competent than he was expecting pirates to be. Much. Who were these people?

Sykora tapped him on the shoulder. "Let's go, Aritza." She encompassed the remaining crew with a look. "Move out."

Javier fell in behind her and tried not to trip over anything as he watched the screen and her butt at the same time. He figured Suvi would warn him if anything really interesting scanned.

Lemuel sat so perfectly still that one of the forest

creatures scampered right past him, chittering angrily just like the squirrel it vaguely resembled. Completely different form, but just as daft.

Below, on the game trail, two people crept past. No, not people. Females. Unclean harlots. Mistresses of Satan. Succubi sent forth to lead the righteous astray into apostasy. He resisted the urge to spit, lest they detect him.

They passed, silent as the wind.

Lemuel didn't bother to follow them. He faded back deeper into the brush. They would seek the wreck, the destruction, the ark that had brought him to this paradise where no females ruled over men unnaturally. He would watch, carefully. There might be others.

DJAMILA KEPT SHARP. The tree-analogs here looked similar and fulfilled the same ecological role. That meant the same propensity for ambush and destruction. She glanced up at Aritza's hovering spy.

She'd had him pull it in close, barely eight meters over her head, despite his grumbling. The scanning range was greatly diminished, but she wanted the extra edge. The woods were populated by a variety of creatures, from birds, to lizards, to things like impalas, to things like bears.

As they moved, she had her safety off. The rest of her crew were fast and good. She was still better. She demanded that extra split-second in an emergency. It might mean the difference between life and death.

Djamila stopped suddenly and pivoted in place. It was an old trick in terrain like this. The sudden turn to catch movement from a watcher giving himself away. Nothing. Well, nothing but Aritza nearly walking into her before he looked up from his screen.

"Hey," he looked up, "a little warning?" He looked extremely put out. She chalked it up to working for so long alone. Probably forgot how to be polite around people. Or maybe he was just an asshole, after all.

She considered growling at him, settled for a sickly-sweet smile instead. The muttering under his breath was reward enough. She smiled to herself and set off again.

Javier set his system to scanning the database of transports, looking for a baseline model to compare against. These things always got customized the second day after they launched, as captains and engineers tweaked things. It would be useful to know what they were working with here. And Yu would appreciate Javier finding him a bigger Auxiliary Power Reactor, to free up space for the next time he had to crawl into the bio-scrubbers.

He was so engrossed in the screen that he stopped ogling Sykora's butt as she moved. And walked right into her when she stopped and looked backwards. Fortunately for his day, he avoided bouncing his nose off of her breast.

"Hey," he looked up, "a little warning?" For a moment, Javier thought she was going to punch him, but she smiled instead. He wasn't sure that it was an improvement, but she started walking again a moment later.

Javier kept his commentary to himself. Mostly.

The emergency beacon had been a standard affair, required by law on every vessel capable of interstellar flight. In this case, it had been the cheapest model on the market, broadcasting a twenty-four digit alpha-numeric ID from the manufacturer, rather than the more sophisticated models that included vessel particulars. That, at least, eliminated several classes of vessels, say, things big enough to have customized beacons, or military vehicles. Javier dug deeper.

At least Sykora warned him before she stopped, the next time. It was the smug smile when he looked up, up, from his screen. He grumbled anyway.

"Rest break here," Sykora called to the group. Everyone else relaxed and looked around the area warily. Things were generally just the wrong-enough shade of green to gnaw at someone.

Javier found a dead tree and sat on the trunk. His least-favorite tree returned to shadow his view.

"Aritza, where are the scouts now?"

He looked up at her sourly.

"Please?" she added quietly. Huh. Old dogs and new tricks. That had sounded almost painful. Still, she sounded sincere. It was certainly the first time he'd ever heard her use that word with him.

Javier toggled one of the side gauges into the projector, zoomed, and washed out small animals. Two dots appeared on the map, plus a few others at a considerable distance. It was a good scanner probe. It helped to have Suvi piloting it and refining the data.

"Three hundred meters out and closing, ma'am," he replied. Teeth were teeth. If she could pull hers and act politely, he could do the same.

She nodded and pulled something from her pocket. She started to put it in her mouth and paused. "Cover your ears, Aritza," she said.

He blinked, thought about it for a half-second, and set the computer down so he could jam fingers in, just before she blew a whistle shrill enough to wake the dead. Hopefully Suvi had been paying attention to the audio channel before it overloaded. Everyone else jumped. Except the other gun bunny. He had apparently known it was coming.

A second sharp blast followed the first.

Javier sat patiently until he saw her put the damned whistle away. A string of curse words appeared on the diagnostics readout at the bottom of the flat screen. Apparently, Suvi had learned some new ones along the way.

Movement at the very edge of the sensor range caught his attention. Looked like a bear from the size and heat signature, but it was moving away from them at a slow amble, so he figured it was safe. Maybe remind everyone to make enough noise to scare off local critters. Last thing he needed right now was angry momma bear.

The two women pathfinders made absolutely no sound.

One minute nothing. Next, they pop out of the brush and stand right next to him. And he'd been watching them approach on the scanner, the last forty meters. What the hell did these people do that they needed these kinds of experts, anyway?

Sykora was in her element. "Status report," she barked.

The shorter of the two, the brunette with the nice hips, came slightly to attention. The blond with the long legs caught him staring and winked.

Javier considered his chances. Might be worth trying.

"We found the wreck, ma'am," Pathfinder Brunette said. "Either there were shipwrecked survivors, or there are locals. We found evidence of habitation."

Javier looked up at the three women. "Bear?"

All three blinked down at him. Apparently they had forgotten he spoke.

"Negative," the brunette said. "Fire pit, hand-made pottery, agriculture, closeable door into a cabin that appears recently used."

"But no one appeared," Sykora stated flatly.

"Affirmative, ma'am," the brunette agreed.

Sykora thought for a second. "Three minute break here,

then we'll push on." The two women dropped in place and pulled out canteens.

The giant redwood tree turned around and looked down at him. "Aritza, push the drone vertical and do that long range scan trick again. I want to see the wreck." Pause. "Please."

The drone took off straight up, but Javier pushed a button on a screen quickly before anyone noticed the discrepancy.

You don't exist, he typed. *Don't anticipate me. These people are smart and dangerous.*

Sorry.

Javier took it up to 200 meters and hovered. One quick rotational scan, and then he focused in on the wreck. This was where Suvi would help.

Hard scan that thing for me. Inventory everything you can. And don't let anything sneak up on us.

Will do, boss.

He poked the volume button and the screen like he was actually controlling it, but he knew Suvi was flying the remote now. After he escaped these yahoos, he might have to upgrade the remote so she could fly it from whatever ship he poured her into next.

And maybe add a gun.

Let's see: two bears, a small herd of elk-like critters, and he was pretty sure that was the local equivalent of a bobcat. Hopefully it wasn't the local version of a wolverine.

Javier looked up at her. "Path's clear," he said, "you might warn people that there are a few dangerous creatures in the woods."

Sykora smiled down at him. "You mean, besides us."

Javier rolled his eyes in pure reflex.

Ogre-lady trying to be funny might be worse than her as a total hard-ass.

He sighed to himself as he stood up. *Another day, another drachma.*

Suvi was torn. On the one hand, it was good to be awake and doing something. On the other hand, she had been weeks off-line. Things had happened, and Javier wasn't filling in the details.

The tall lady seemed to be in charge. And scary. Suvi really needed her processing core to read the inter-personal dynamics playing out around her. The chip she was on was barely big enough to hold her personality and near-term memory.

As it was, she'd had to off-load some of her consciousness onto the portable. There was certainly space for files, but the processor on that thing was horribly under-powered. She was almost thinking at human speeds. Egads. How did they operate so slow?

She spun the remote in place and pinged. Precious few birds, none of them big enough to threaten her new little flitter-ship. Some fauna large enough to maybe be dangerous, depending on how this planet had evolved.

Over there, some fields had been planted with human-digestible crops, so someone had survived the crash and broken out the emergency seed packet. And it had worked for them, if they'd been here for seventeen years.

Quick pass through the memory files of the remote. The wreck looked kinda like a Kallasky Engineering Mark IX Conestoga. Big, slow, durable. Too many pieces to be sure until she could read some part numbers off the engine, or they found the nameplate.

Suvi counted her humans. Javier, Tall Lady, two "pathfinders" (note: look that term up when connected to better resources. Got no useful dictionary here.), one heavily-armed male, one male and one female without arms, but with toolkits. (note: mark the latter tentatively as engineering crew. Update later. Ask Javier.)

She needed better information. She was missing too much. Javier had said to hide, so she decided to play along. Happy little flying mouse, zooming overhead.

She aimed her microphones down, but Javier grumbling to himself seemed to be the only conversation.

Who were these people?

LEMUEL WATCHED the wreck from a nearby hilltop. He felt sure he was supposed to be overjoyed by the arrival of people. It would be possible to leave this world and return to civilization.

Did he want to?

The ancients had venerated the ascetics, monks living on the edges of the desert, praying and fasting, living holy lives of contemplation.

He had not intended to crash here. But once it was done, he had put in a great deal of contemplation on the Lord's message to him. The Harlot was not meant to rule over men. So she had not. The others had not seen it that way. They had joined her. It was the way of things.

And now, he could return to the world.

But would he have to sacrifice holiness? More harlots had come. One seemed to rule them.

She would have to go.

But the others?

He would have to get closer to see how many of them would trod the path of the righteous. Many were incapable of enlightenment.

The silver bird troubled him.

It flew wrong, was shaped wrong, was wrong. Lemuel knew his eyes were old, but he remembered technology. The silver bird was a device, a thing. It had eyes to watch. He could not sneak up on them unaware. He would have to gain their confidence.

Lemuel silently rose to his feet and took a step down the hillside. It was irrational, but he could feel the silver bird's eyes on him immediately.

So be it. He would be friendly and thankful to his rescuers.

Then he would kill them.

***

SUVI UNDERSTOOD the need for silence, but she really wished she could talk to Javier. Text lacked the subtleties. She settled for highlighting a dot on the display. **That's not a bear**.

She pinged it, hard, once, with every sensor the little flitter-ship had. Yup. Definitely human. Male. Mid-fifties. Pretty good shape if he was a shipwrecked survivor deep into his second decade of local realtime. She displayed his stats.

Javier's voice on the portable's audio input. "Sykora," he said. "Company."

Suvi watched the two armed humans point rifles in opposite directions immediately. The two pathfinder women drew sidearms as well, squatting down and aiming outward. The two engineers dropped to the ground without a word. Javier just stood there.

Tall Lady spoke. "Where?"

Javier glanced at the screen, turned to his right, and waved with a cheery, "Good morning."

Tall Lady was aghast. "What are you doing, Aritza?" she queried. A moment later, she called, "Flip."

Suvi watched her and the armed male change sides of coverage like a ballet, leaving the one called Sykora pointed where Javier was looking and the other covering the "rear."

The strange human was approaching slowly, quietly. He wore robes made of a rough, homespun cotton, probably locally grown from seedstock, and carried a walking stick.

She bounced the flitter-ship up higher for a better view and scanned everything once, and then dropped down close.

Finally, she might get some answers.

JAVIER CONSIDERED THE DEAD FREIGHTER. Definitely came in too hot. Looks like it tore off a landing skid on that rock, which dropped the bow into the ground at speed, which cracked her spine there and there. Probably one you walked away from, unless your number had come up.

Reactor was definitely on-line, banked to minimum load. Heat and light leaked out of an open hatch and the cooling fins were well above ambient temperature.

Somebody lived here. A field of human crops close to harvest. A small drying shed filled with…stuff. Dunno what else to call it. A path down to the stream below. Homey. Javier could see himself living here and enjoying the place. Clean air. No people. Paradise.

That's not a bear.

Good thing Suvi was on the job.

Might as well start the fun. "Sykora," he said. "Company."

Javier watched the armed lunatics go into full combat mode. This was why he was a civilian now. That kind of thinking was just bad. Desperately anti-social.

Sykora was the worst. "Where?" She was probably planning a firefight right about now.

Javier really needed some coffee.

He turned to his right, and waved, "Good morning."

Behind him, he was pretty sure he could hear teeth grind. "What are you doing, Aritza?" Ogre lady snarled at him. A moment later, "Flip."

Great, now she was standing next to him, hovering over his shoulder, big honking war machine ready to lay the smack-down.

I got out of bed this morning for this?

Javier pointed. "A guy. The survivor, I'm guessing. And we're in his front yard, so maybe we should be nice to him?"

Javier slid out of reach and stepped forward. Good old-fashioned Biblical Patriarch stepped into view, complete with a beard to his waist and the sort of stick Moses carried in every video Javier'd ever seen of Exodus. In a dark alley, he might be scary. Here? Faced by a small army? Harmless.

"I'm Javier," he addressed the newcomer. "We saw your signal. Took a while. You are most definitely in the middle of absolutely nowhere."

The man considered him silently. Which made sense. Javier had months where the only person he talked to besides the chickens was Suvi. The old man might have forgotten how to talk. Or, maybe he spoke something really obscure and didn't grok.

What the hell. Javier reached into his pack and pulled out a bar of dried fruit and oats. He opened the bar and held it out as a peace offering. "Food?"

A hand descended from the heavens and drug him back a step before the man moved. Javier hadn't forgotten how strong Sykora was. But, man…

"What the hell do you think you're doing, Aritza?"

Javier turned. Nobody was sneaking up on these people,

so he could ignore the guy. "Diplomacy, lady," he said with an exasperated sigh. "Being nice. It's the part of negotiations that doesn't involve shooting people."

She was back to staring daggers. "I'm in charge here." That tone might have put an edge on a dull knife.

Fine. "Fine," Javier said. What the hell. He plopped down, crossed his legs, and took a bite of the bar. Let the gun bunny sort it out.

She snarled down at him. "Now what are you doing?" Javier noted that at no point did the barrel ever waver from dead-center on the new guy. Pissed, she might be. Deadly, without a doubt.

"You're in charge, Sykora," he snarled back, only a little less hostile. "Do it your way."

YES, that was the way of things, Lemuel thought. The Harlot was not suited to lead. She knew only violence or seduction. Not the ways of Men. Here, She was surrounded by sycophants, but for one who was not under her spell. Lemuel found that his purpose was clear.

He relaxed his natural scowl and tried to remember how to smile. The Harlot was a lost cause, so he directed it at the man sitting. "He-he-hello," he stuttered.

He found speech to be a complicated task, once the habit was lost. He spent most of his weeks in silent prayer and the sort of hard work necessary to survive in the Lord's paradise.

The Harlot kept her weapon pointed at him. And her bile.

"What's your name?" she challenged him.

That brought Lemuel up short. He hadn't used his name in...a very long time. He blinked a few times. How many seasons had he been here? Many, doing the Lord's work in the wilderness.

"Answer me," the Harlot continued, her anger palpable.

The Lord counseled patience in the face of the denizens of the pit. "Le-Lemuel," he said brokenly, finding the word deep in his memory.

The friendly male, unbowed by the Harlot, spoke to him from the dirt. "Hungry?"

Lemuel cocked his head. Words were difficult to process.

"Here," the man continued. He held out his hand, holding the bar of food that he had taken a bite from.

The Harlot's fury grew. "Come no closer," she rasped harshly.

The male looked up at her, rolled his eyes disapprovingly, and tossed the bar to Lemuel with a single, "Fine. Catch."

Lemuel managed to keep it from falling.

A sniff. A blue and red thing. Fruit of some sort, dried and packed together, with nuts he could not recognize. Minus a healthy bite out of one end.

Since it came from the male, Lemuel broke off a small chunk and touched it with his tongue. The poisons in this place were subtle, but dangerous. Mohr had died after eating the local fruit in an attempt to go native on this world.

Thus did the Righteous fall from the Lord's Grace.

Lemuel took a very small bite. Better to risk illness than to refuse his one potential ally among the strangers and burn a valuable bridge. He considered his words as he slowly chewed.

"Thank you," he finally found. Language was coming back to him now.

Lemuel considered the lovely taste, fruits that would not grow in this Eden, nuts from alien trees. His body remembered the taste of honey, so different from the form the local insects made.

Perhaps the Lord was telling him that he could finally go home, after so long in the wilderness.

The Harlot would not be an easy foe.

The words of his father came back to him, across the gulf of vast time.

"Welcome," he said slowly, carefully, enunciating each word with care. "Welcome to Eden."

Djamila was not taken in by the rustic's pose. He had already survived many years on the surface of a hostile planet, surrounded by alien flora and fauna. That made him dangerous. That Eden nonsense bullshit wasn't going to cut it.

And Aritza was going to play good cop. Big surprise there. The man had no sense. None.

Predictable. But she could bad cop with the best of them. Watch this.

"Aritza," she called down to the punk sitting in the dirt, "Is he armed?"

"No." The answer was surprisingly quick. And assured.

"How do you know?" she asked.

"Because," he replied in a voice right at the edge of insubordinate, "the only power sources that aren't over here are in that." A finger pointed at the wreck. "My sensors showed him as a bear until he came into the open."

"And the staff he's carrying?"

"What?" Aritza shot back. "You can't take an old man with a stick?"

Djamila considered kicking him. Aritza was really getting on her nerves.

She scowled her best, most professional, scowl at the

native. Yes, she could handle him unarmed. Plus, she was supposed to be nice.

Interstellar law and custom said you always rescued ship-wrecked survivors and got them back to civilization. Even pirates honored that one. Mostly.

So, catalog the wreck. Rescue the local. Figure out if she could make it look like a tragic accident had killed Aritza.

She slung the battle-rifle on her shoulder.

All in a day's work.

JAVIER WATCHED Sykora's face on the sly.

He thought about teaching her how to play poker one of these days, but decided he was safer not telling her she was an open book. The Gunners on B deck were more fun, anyway.

The old man stared intently at him, waiting for the other shoe to drop. Better poker player there. Didn't like Sykora at all. That made him good people.

Might as well cut straight to the messy bits.

Javier levered himself upright and brushed the dirt and leaves and crap off his butt with one hand. He clicked the recall button on the portable and caught the remote as it settled into his hand. Suvi would keep it active. She was very smart. Much better to trust her than the ogre-lady.

Now, the old man.

"So the reason we came here was to salvage the wreck, Lemuel," he said. Simple. Honest. Easy. "We didn't expect to find anyone alive after all this time."

Javier read the signs as he spoke. Two guys at a bus stop, talking about last night's game. He waited for Lemuel's nod, got it, went on.

"Interstellar law says we rescue you at this point and get

you someplace where you can get home from." Javier turned as he spoke and looked right up at Sykora's scowl. "Where and how will be up to Captain Sokolov, but you'll be able to save some of your stuff."

Again, the pause as Lemuel processed his words and nodded.

"We're going to inventory everything for value, and most definitely remove the power reactor. What was on your manifest?"

He watched Lemuel scrunch up his face in thought. The eyes drifted off focus and blinked rapidly. A hand came up and scratched the semi-bald pate. Javier heard him whisper *Home* once, under his breath. A very small smile appeared briefly.

The eyes finally focused on his. "Um. Machine parts, I think," Lemuel said quietly. "And trade goods for some colony."

Sykora overrode his next question. "Which colony?" she barked.

Lemuel looked down, apparently embarrassed. "I do not know," he said. "I was a cook and stevedore. Anya was the navigator."

Javier turned to Sykora and gave her his best stink-eye scowl. Then a smile as he turned back to the old man. "So let's go take a tour of the wreck, Lemuel," he said soothingly. "You can point out all the interesting and dangerous parts as we go."

This was going to be like herding cats. Normally, Javier would have said herding goldfish, but carp won't turn suddenly and slash you with their claws. Sykora had that look in her eyes.

PART FOUR

Lemuel considered his options as they ascended into the ship. They were many, but he bestrode a dangerous path.

Javier had introduced himself and made it clear that he could become a friend.

The Harlot had a name as well, but Lemuel had not bothered to remember it. Weren't they all the same, after all?

The others, male and female alike, were obviously under the sway of the Harlot. From the looks and mannerisms, Lemuel could see that they considered Javier an outsider to their group, though they treated him with respect.

That gave him an opening. Did he have the courage to seize it? Was this place to become Megiddo, after all? The Lord had worked in his mysterious ways to place Lemuel here so long ago.

Had he finally proven the strength of his faith? Or had he failed and was to be irrevocably damned by the Harlot?

Lemuel prayed silently to himself as he led the troupe of strangers, invaders unto his quiet paradise, down into the realm of his earliest, greatest challenge.

Suvi was having an adventure.

The flitter-ship was far more maneuverable than *Mielikki* had been. She could hover, and spin, and bob, and float, and saunter. She missed having a turret she could use, but on a hull this small, it probably wouldn't do more than irritate a squirrel. Not that that was a bad thing.

She had already used a series of ultrasound pings to map the hallway and the first cargo hold they had entered. The humans hadn't heard, but they missed everything anyway.

Now she was studying a small lizard-looking creature on a wall. Maybe the philosophical offspring of a gecko and a chameleon. It blended well, but moved quickly and gracefully. And couldn't have been more than six centimeters long.

She watched it munch happily on the local equivalent of a spider that hadn't heard him coming either. There was probably a moral to that story.

Suvi launched another aggressive series of pings, but nothing moved.

She flitted over to a crate and scanned the weathered coding on the side. The language of shipping containers was probably the first universal stellar language. You could write and speak in any number of tongues and get by, but you had to talk to a very limited intelligence computer to move big things around.

That meant simple codes, with descriptive tags built in, so that someone could point a laser scanner at a stack of containers, scan the whole wall, and inventory everything in seconds. Here, she was stuck thinking at almost human speeds, so it took much longer, and the flitter-ship had a very limited scanning laser, so she had to get close.

But it was fun.

This one contained quality glasswork, cups and vases and such, designed to be sold boutique-style on a frontier colony with some money. The sort of place that had been too poor to take anything initially that wasn't directly related to immediate survival. And had then survived the first few years in the wilderness, and prospered enough that people were ready to have nice things. Suvi added it to the list.

There weren't any great prizes here. No precious metal alloys, or objets d'art, or high-end machine parts that Javier could use to build her a new ship. And this freighter was never flying again without more time in a space-dock than was worth considering. From what she had overheard, the others were mostly interested in ripping out the reactors and engines anyway.

Then she remembered the Black Flag. Being stuck thinking at only human speeds really sucked. These people were the pirates who had jumped them. Javier was a prisoner, of sorts, and that's why they thought she was dead.

Duh.

Gods, she hated slow processing hardware.

Well, that changed everything. If Javier was working with them, he had some sort of deal going, and she was his ace in the hole. She could do that.

Now she really missed all the extra brain horsepower. It would be nice to be able to read these people at the unconscious level, with all sorts of extra scanners and thermometers so she had a solid hold on their biometrics. Hmmm. She'd have to settle for turning up the audio channels and putting in a cutout in case it got loud suddenly.

Time to watch, and wait, and prepare. Javier was going to need her.

JAVIER SMILED BUT GRUMBLED. Having an honest deal with a bunch of pirates was one thing, but it would have been nice if this wreck had had some sort of big score. If he had to work with Sykora for four years, one of them would end up messily dead. No doubt about that.

He was under no illusion that he'd have any chance to escape or communicate with anybody, any time they got close to civilization. Even with a lot of planning. Ogre Lady would just lock him in a broom closet for a day if she had to.

And the old man was going to be no help at all. He seemed lost in a fugue of some sort. Probably spent too long alone here and gone totally nuts. He certainly didn't realize he mumbled, not that anything coherent came out.

And Sykora…Yeah. Don't let her too close behind you. Simple as that. At least he had Suvi watching his back. Not that she could do much, but she was going to make his work a whole lot easier while he was here. And she could keep his back safer.

Javier watched as another box came up on the screen, inventoried, mapped, and tagged. If nothing else, at least they had something to show for all the effort.

He was going to be too busy just staying alive. Being Science Officer could wait.

DJAMILA WAS TORN. The freighter was completely indefensible from even the most rudimentary approach. She had already passed seven places where she would have secured a door, prepared an ambush point, or built a trap. This person, this local with the hard eyes, was a complete amateur. On the other hand, it would make things easier if she found it necessary to arrange accidents for several people down here.

At least one of them deserved it. She was even trying to be nice. Aritza just pushed her buttons. She hadn't even pushed back. Yet.

At least the trip was a success. Based on the manifests alone, if even a third of the cargo survived, they could sell it for a profit, over and above getting a new power reactor. The Captain would be pleased.

She watched Aritza and the local confer on something. It involved a lot of pointing on Aritza's part, and shrugs in response. Much as she hated to admit it, the punk had an easy way with people. Much like the Captain did. She had never gotten the hang of it, and, until now, never really appreciated how useful a tool it could be in her inventory.

Huh. Perhaps the old bitch dog needed to learn a new trick or two. It galled her to think Aritza had something useful to teach her. But there it was.

All right. Observe. Understand. Learn.

No different than taking a fortified position away from bad guys. Figure out their weak point. Come at them sidelong. Get the mission done before they can respond. Tactical 101.

Djamila walked up on the conversation at a measured pace. Quiet. Dignified. Prepared. Open.

Aritza had apparently developed a sixth sense regarding her. He seemed to place her physically at all times, even when he wasn't looking. She felt a moment of thrill course through her for no good reason. No, there was a reason. For all his nonchalance, he was acutely aware of her, even subconsciously, and paying extra special attention.

Good. That meant she had gotten through to him, at least at some level.

Javier registered Sykora before he realized she was that close behind him. Nobody that big should be allowed to move that quietly.

And yet, his favorite tree had sprung up behind him, listening to things without interrupting. It must have galled the control-freak in her to sit passively. Good. Do her good to be in a situation where she wasn't completely in control. Maybe she'd learn to be human occasionally.

He glanced back once. Well, up and back. Seriously, unless she was this close, he forgot just how big she was. Perfectly proportioned woman, just a whole head taller than him. Dancing with her would be fun. Distracting, but fun.

And she didn't say anything. Just hovered in that perfectly poised way she moved. Like she was expecting bad guys to come out of the air vents at any moment, or something. It would involve guns. She did guns well.

But she didn't say anything. Just watched him like a hawk. Weird. Most women nattered. Not her. Didn't even fidget. Might have been carved in white marble. Artemis, by Michelangelo. Huh.

Javier went right ahead with his own nattering. Lemuel seemed a good enough guy. Little lonely. Hard time remembering words. Seventeen years of solo survival on a hostile planet would do that. He himself usually needed a few days in a bar before people made sense again, once he got back from one of his long runs in the darkness.

The cargo was in good enough shape, as the hull had largely held, except where it had cracked on the frames, but that let weather in between spaces instead of into them. Javier figured they would make a clearing and drop the shuttle into it, next trip, so they could pull the reactor and haul it the shortest distance. Maybe the engines were salvageable as well. Hadn't made it that far. And the corvette didn't need them, but there was enough space on the flight deck for another small ship, a gunboat, or a scout.

If he was going to be stuck with these yahoos for a while, he might as well make it as profitable as possible. Buy his freedom, make his escape, whatever.

It would involve these people getting what they deserved. He was sure of that.

* * *

LEMUEL FOUGHT to keep his face and mannerisms passive when the eureka moment struck him. For better than an hour, he had explained long forgotten things to the strangers. Well, to Javier. The rest had just trailed along quietly, not touching much, but paying way too much attention to everything around them except him.

By now, he was pretty sure they were pirates. But Javier wasn't one of *them*. Just along for the ride, somehow. Perhaps a prisoner, based on one of his off-hand comments.

Lemuel considered that The Lord might have finally decided he had been tempered enough by the wilderness. Perhaps it was time to take his message to the broader universe. Lemuel had never considered himself a prophet. But it was apparently time.

The Harlot would be the biggest problem. The Lord had put her there as his final challenge before he could bring enlightenment to the galaxy. Well enough. He would overcome her.

She would not be an easy foe. But The Lord had never intended his to be an easy life. And Javier would only be able to help a little. Less, if he was a prisoner and needed to be kept ignorant.

But The Lord would provide.

He continued to answer questions from Javier, even as a

supernova exploded in his brain. He could do this. And make it look like a terrible accident.

The Harlot would be first, as she deserved, followed by the three other harlots. And the rest of the Harlot's followers. Only Javier would escape. For now. Perhaps he would have to be sacrificed for the greater good later. The Lord would make His will known when the time was right.

Suvi flitter-shipped up and over the wreck. After two hours down in the bowels of the dead freighter, she needed a breath of fresh air and some open skies. Even if she was an AI.

Below, Javier seemed happy, overall. Somewhere, recently, a secondary power reactor had made him extremely angry. She could tell by the way his voice grated when it came up. The wreck was going to make it all better, somehow.

Tall Lady, the one called Sykora, appeared pleased as well, so maybe they knew a place they could sell the cargo.

The survivor, Lemuel, was harder to read. She had studied his face. It went from happy to angry and back quickly, but most of the time it was placid. Suvi'd be happy to get her poker-playing sub-routines back on line, so she could understand better all the subtle byplay going on. She wasn't close enough to human to just read them and understand what wasn't being said.

For now, she scanned the few lizard-birds in the neighborhood. Nothing larger than a house cat was within a kilometer of the shipwreck. Somewhere, over behind that hill, somebody named Del was listening to weird music in the background, when Sykora checked in every fifteen minutes. And he was very bored.

Suvi checked her power levels. Enough flight for several hours. More if she kept the scanning to a minimum and sat on a flat rock somewhere, absorbing sunlight. She found a nice spot above the bow of the broken freighter and settled.

The sun felt good on her back. She dialed up the audio sensors to their highest gain and sunbathed while she waited for Javier to call.

LEMUEL WAS on firmer ground now. The strangers had completed their tour of the ship and were making plans to salvage everything so they could haul it back to civilization, including him. The Lord was finally calling him to service.

They sat in the clearing below his crude cabin and broke out pre-fabricated meal packets for themselves. Javier had offered him one, and shown him how to activate the heating element. The smell was nearly overwhelming, as he had not had any meat to eat in many, many years.

None of the animals on this planet could be safely consumed. Even most of the plants were harmful.

Thus had The Lord make his displeasure with Mohr known.

There was a plant Lemuel had found safe, at least for him. Over the years, he had developed something of an resistance to the trace alkaloids in the leaves, if he boiled them long enough into a tea. His dreams were deep and bizarre afterwards, but he was mostly immune now.

Thus had The Lord delivered into his hands the tools of His vengeance on The Harlot.

Lemuel concentrated on his tea kettle, hanging over the

fire on salvaged iron bars. As long as the water was boiled hard and rolled, everything dangerous in it was likely killed. He felt Javier's gaze.

"So, Lemuel," Javier asked him, "are the local plants and animals edible?"

Lemuel scowled, mostly to himself. "There are a few safe plants," he said, skirting the trust carefully in his service to The Lord. "The animals are too dangerous to eat. We did not have the tools to understand that when we crashed. Mohr died of the poison. Thomas was killed by a fever."

Javier processed all that carefully. "And Anya, the pilot?"

Lemuel shrugged, skating carefully around the truth. "Her death is why we crashed here," he said, obliquely. "None but her could fly the ship, and the computer was not up to the task."

Lemuel left off the bashed-in skull that had caused Anya's death. They would not understand that she was a Harlot that had deserved death, like so many others that exercised power over him in defiance of The Lord's **Will**.

The whistling steam precluded conversation for a moment. Lemuel felt many eyes upon him. He realized, belatedly, that the simple act of boiling water in an iron pot might be something none but him had ever seen or done. Javier seemed to understand, but he wasn't of *them*.

Lemuel concentrated on turning the simple ritual of tea into a performance.

Let the water boil for several long moments for safety. The local animals had a tendency to flee at the sound. The humans just watched him, rapt.

Pull the kettle from the hanging iron with a cozy he had knitted the third winter, when he began to make his own cloth from cotton he grew and harvested. Rest it on the warm flat rock placed there for just this reason.

Put his largest soup pot next to the kettle on the rock.

Pour a bit of boiled water in and swirl it around to clean and sterilize things.

Pour the cleaning water over the composting pile to keep things damp for the digesting bacteria.

Add several measures of the dried leaves he called *Dream Tea* to the soup pot and pour most of the hot water over it. Retain some of the boiled water to clean the pot later, after reheating.

Stir vigorously for a few seconds to unsettle everything.

And then several minutes of patience as the tea steeped. For Lemuel, a ritual nearly as important as thrice-daily prayer. Cleanliness was next to godliness, especially in this place where so many poisonous things waited to trip the unwary.

Around him, the unwary awaited their fate blindly.

The Lord would welcome them.

JAVIER BIT BACK A LAUGH. For people raised on food-dispenser computers, tea-making probably looked a lot like magic. He would know. He had done it enough times, usually for station commanders and admirals.

And Lemuel seemed to have something of the showman in him, after all. Javier watched him rise to the occasion of good performance art.

The tea smelled good, too. Earthy and rich in a way that chemically-processed stuff never had. Javier bit back a moment of frustration and rage at the fate of *Mielikki*. At least he had saved all the botany. And hopefully Yu was keeping the chickens as happy as they ever got.

All in all, things could have been much worse.

Lemuel found that The Lord had granted his prayers for calmness and patience today.

The tea reached a point of inflection, like a magical infusion of happiness and psychedelic nocturne.

He ladled himself a small cup and tasted it. Perfect. Light enough that he would be happy all day, but not enough to overwhelm him with the sort of sleepiness that had visited him in the early days, before he had developed much immunity.

Lemuel refilled his cup and set it to one side.

He looked up at the surrounding group and smiled. The Lord had indeed provided.

Lemuel gestured with the pot. "My friends, I would like to share with you something of this world that I will soon be departing. It has brought me much joy and calmness over the years. I think you will enjoy it as well."

The others smiled up at him. Even the Harlot relaxed her eternal vigilance and hostility. Lemuel considered that the greatest sign yet. "Please join me in a toast."

Javier held out a mug that Lemuel filled. Lemuel watched him take the smallest taste with a knowing twinkle in his eye.

Truly, Lemuel had found his ally against the Harlot. They would join forces and kill all the pirates, and then go forth and wreak a terrible vengeance on the universe together.

He smiled as he carried the pot around to each of the invaders and shared with them their own taste of The Lord's wrath.

Something about the whole situation just felt off. Javier couldn't put his finger on it, but Lemuel just felt wrong. All too pleased with himself. Not nearly uptight enough for so many strangers around, or the impending upset to his life. Even rescue didn't explain it.

Javier took just enough of the tea to get a taste, while pretending to take a reasonable drink. He knew better than to try anything on a strange planet.

Yup. Something there. A trace of…*what*? Most of the pirates might have tried various narcotics over the years, licit and otherwise, but probably none of them had made a scientific event of it. Certainly one that certain Shore Patrols still talked about, years later.

Their lives rarely depended on that sort of thing.

His did.

So. Accidental drug overdose, or deliberate? The man's behavior just didn't ring right. Probably not an accident, then. Still, this felt more like a narcotic than a poison.

He should probably do something about it. At least it wasn't that toxic, if this Lemuel-dude was willing to drink it. Slow acting at least, probably not lethal.

It would be impolite to tell the dragon-lady if he was wrong. She'd just shoot the guy out of hand and be done with it. Maybe he didn't deserve that. Maybe he did. You never knew.

Fortunately, Javier was prepared for this sort of thing. These people had no clue what to do on the surface of a hostile world. Obviously, they needed a Science Officer to keep them alive.

Next question, did he want them alive?

Most of them were just folks, doing what they needed to do to get through their day. Not particularly evil or vile creatures.

Sykora, on the other hand…Yeah, he owed her a few. Be interesting to wind her sideways on a good hallucinogenic sometime. Might even make her tolerable. Maybe he should try it. She seemed like she was trying to be nicer than she had been.

Ah, what the hell.

Javier picked up the portable and started typing. He had an expert handy. Let her do the heavy lifting.

Suvi, I know you are in range. Please scan the tea with your laser spectrograph and let me know your results. Quietly.

Javier smiled. One of the new berry species he was exploring had originally been evolved from something called Moroccan Dreamberries. Maybe he needed to spend some time breeding a few crops back into the mother line and see if he could amp up some of the more interesting chemical signatures.

Hell, Sykora might even smile.

Around him, the crew smiled and toasted with the poisoned tea. They didn't seem to notice the slightly metallic taste underneath, but they weren't used to living with this level of paranoia.

Nobody was.

Javier watched Sykora drain her mug in a single shot. It was larger than everyone else's, but she was a big girl. Javier was really, really torn.

He faked taking another sip.

Sykora rapped her cup lightly to get the dude's attention with a "more, please," as well. Please? That was kinda scary, coming out of her mouth without being drug by horses.

As Lemuel stepped around to pour her more tea, Javier surreptitiously poured his cup out on the ground and shifted a heel over it to cover the mud until it soaked into the ground.

His portable computer beeped with a message.

Please tell me you didn't drink any of the tea. Scan identifies trace amides of ergoline present. Expect psycho-

chemically-induced hallucinations, possibly with additional soporific qualities. *** DANGEROUS!!! ***

Javier grinned to himself. Rapid acid trip and a nap. Not necessarily a bad thing, if he was in a controlled setting with people he trusted, or locked in a small hotel room by himself. At least it hadn't been bad last time.

This time was gonna be different. Javier doubted that the local was unaware of the effects of his tea on people. So what was Lemuel going to do about it? And, more importantly, what should he do?

———

LEMUEL WORKED VERY hard to keep a smile on his face as everyone drank the dreaming tea, including the three lesser harlots and the spawn of the unnameable Dark One who led them. Sleep would take them soon, darkness tinged with terror and no escape. Then, he would begin his crusade into the broader universe.

And, as a bonus, the friendly one, Javier, was going to help him kill these people.

From the corner of an eye, Lemuel had watched Javier pour out his tea instead of drinking it. He had known a moment of panic as he stood before The Harlot with all her guns, attempting to be calm while pouring, but Javier had remained silent.

It was a *Sign*.

Lemuel returned to his spot by the small fire and sat the kettle down, listening to the ribald banter flowing back and forth between the strangers. The Dreaming would take them soon. All he had to do was wait, and offer up a small prayer to The Lord for the souls that he was about to send to their final resting place.

Already the tea took its toll. The least harlot was slumped

in on herself, precariously balanced with her head down, ripe for the slightest nudge to fall over.

Lemuel smiled.

The heavily armed male was next. Even from here, Lemuel could see his pupils begin to dilate as his speech became labored. In the middle of a word, his brain passed the threshold into sleep. He fell against one of the harlots in green and collapsed atop her in a crude approximation of mating.

Lemuel held his breath as he counted bodies. All were down, save for Javier his friend, and The Harlot who was his adversary's very avatar on Earth. And even she was on the final stages of crisis. He could see the painful realization of failure take hold of her mind, shackled by the twin narcotic hammers of sleep and nightmare, beating away at her walls.

Lemuel knew a moment of total panic as she rose to her knees and drew one of her weapons, pin-prick eyes locked on him like a missile. Before he could move, the weapon came up. Lemuel held his breath.

The shot stirred a puff of dirt between them as darkness claimed her. The Harlot crumpled face down, her very will defeated, the pistol fallen before his Adversary could strike.

Hers would be a quick, painless death. He owed her that much.

Lemuel reached down and picked up one of the rocks that marked the boundary of his fire pit. It was hot to the touch, but he did not feel it. In his mind, he could already see skulls caved in under the fierce impact of this stone. The Lord had spoken to him.

It would be like before. Anya dead on the deck, her blood splattered randomly on the walls in a message he had spent seventeen years trying to decipher. Thomas and Mohr aghast, but unwilling to challenge him. Escape across several systems until they were safe from pursuit and could live out their lives as men, without the creeping infestation of the harlots turning them from the path of righteousness.

Lemuel smiled and hefted the rock. The Harlot would be first to die. She could lead her troop into hell personally. He took a step forward to begin the crusade.

"I wouldn't do that, if I were you…"

Javier felt like a shit.

Here, he's spent weeks dreaming of ways to get even with Sykora for all the things she'd done to him. Planning ways he could escape and bring down the full force of the *Concord* Fleet on these bastards, hang them from the highest yardarm, pay them back for Suvi and *Mielikki*.

And now, here he was.

He watched the local dude count them falling with a smile on his face. Okay, so not an accidental overdose, after all.

The rock was a very bad sign. It meant things were about to get stupid.

Javier considered the man. Half a head taller than him. Maybe an extra ten kilos of mass. And right now, the sort of crazy fire in the eyes that just meant everything was about to go to hell. He'd finally figured out that look with his second ex-wife.

Still, Javier was twenty years younger, and had kept up his close combat training over the years. He should be able to take this guy.

Time to save the crew from their own innocent stupidity.

"I wouldn't do that, if I were you," Javier announced in the sort of voice he always heard in the videos. *Never thought I'd be able to actually say that in a real situation.*

He watched Lemuel turn stupidly to stare at him, a

jagged five-kilo rock in one hand like a primitive ape's hammer.

"Javier?" the guy was confused, and maybe a bit put out.

"I can't let you kill these people, Lemuel," Javier continued, trying to be soothing. "Drop the rock and we'll make sure you get back to civilization and get the treatment you need. I realize you've been out here a long time and kinda gone stale. We can help."

Javier watched, hopeful, as the crazy seemed to ebb in the guy's eyes, just for a second. Maybe he could talk his way out of this, after all.

And then the fire came back, twice as nuts. "No," Lemuel roared, "The Harlot must die. All harlots must be destroyed if men are to achieve righteousness. So sayeth The Lord."

Javier watched as the man turned, ignoring him, and reared back with the rock, poised over Sykora's unconscious form.

Shit.

Javier took two running steps and tackled the man before Lemuel could crush Sykora's skull. He landed on top of the guy and got in a couple of good body blows. That just seemed to piss him off.

Javier had never understood the term until now, thought it was a joke. *Rage Strength*. Lemuel took him by surprise. The man flipped him backwards with two hands to the chest, leaving Javier suddenly on his back a meter away.

And then the gorilla was on him. They traded punches. Javier felt his brain rattle around inside his skull. Lemuel didn't seem to notice. Okay, not good.

Javier hooked the lunatic with his foot, twisted them both until he ended up on top. One. Two. Three shots to the side of the head. That just seemed to make him angrier. *Crap*. Was this guy made of brick? That always worked in the movies.

Two big gorilla hands came up and grabbed Javier's throat. Air suddenly became a commodity. Javier shifted, tried to break loose.

Lemuel twisted him, shook him like a rag doll. Suddenly he was face up in the dirt again.

Lemuel stared down with a fiery rage as his hands continued to squeeze. "Why, Javier?" he raged. "She is The Harlot. She is Evil's Mistress. Her kind must be destroyed. You could have helped me, joined me. WHY?"

Movement out of the corner of his eye as things started to get black. Javier smiled into the face of death. Lemuel had longer arms, but Javier could still rabbit punch him in the ribs, keep his attention focused down here, keep him really angry. Not that that was hard to do. Just stay awake a little longer. *I can do that.*

"Because," Javier said calmly, timing it just like in all the movies he'd ever seen, "because it's wrong."

The remote slammed into the side of Lemuel's head at full speed with a thunderous crack. Javier felt the man go slack as he slid to one side under the tremendous kick. Lemuel flopped over and lay next to him in the dirt.

Unlike Javier, however, he was no longer breathing.

SUVI CURSED like a sailor as she ran diagnostics on her flitter-ship. Almost everything was off-line, broken. At least she had rolled to a stop face up, although she could imagine a human would have been puking her guts up flipping that many times in a gravity well.

This was the second ship Javier had cost her. He was going to owe her. Big.

She watched him stagger to his feet, take two steps over to the portable computer and start punching keys.

Whatever he was typing, it had better be good. I'm stuck over here and this thing's nearly broken. You owe me.

Suvi pouted.

Thank you for saving my life.

Oh. Well then, that made it all right.

Suvi smiled.

PART SIX

Javier rapped on the closed door twice. Inside, a muffled "Enter," and the door slid aside. He peeked into the small chamber.

Sykora's cabin was stark and nearly bare. A desk, a tall locker shut tight, a bed. No pictures, no color, no scent, nothing. Stark, bare metal. The only hint of personality to be found was a ball of yarn, knitting needles, and something that might be half of a scarf, balled up next to her on the bed.

She was stretched out in her day uniform, ship slippers on her feet, boots lined up at the foot of the bed. She had been reading something on a portable screen, but she powered it off and set it to one side when she recognized him.

"What is it, Aritza?" she asked. There was still an edge to her voice, but it was more tired and less grumpy than last week.

Javier hoped.

He leaned on the door after it closed, unwilling to enter any deeper into her sanctuary than necessary. Without her riding his ass all the time, he had time to do some research on her past.

Neu Berne society had proved to be quite interesting on further reading. He was already verging on impolite, just by being here in her cabin, uninvited, but didn't want to have this conversation anywhere else on the ship, especially not where anyone could overhear.

Javier took a breath.

He'd come here to talk about nice things. Letting bygones be bygones. Stuff like that.

The speech he had planned already sounded wrong, so he tossed it aside and looked at her. Really looked at her. "I wanted to see how you were doing. Medbot said you got an extra hard dose of the stuff that lunatic tried to poison everyone with."

He watched her bite back something sharp and sarcastic. It left a bilious taste in the air, but went unsaid, so it could be ignored. That was already an improvement, considering Sykora. She took a breath, looked down uncomfortably, fought visibly for the words.

Awkward moments passed.

"I think," she said finally, "that the worst has passed." She breathed. "According to the system, I will continue to have chemically-induced nightmares for several weeks, but I should be cleared for duty tomorrow."

Javier nodded. "That's good. We've missed you on the bridge."

She rewarded him with a bleak, wan smile. "I'm sure, Aritza," she said. "Always a party with you."

Javier bit back his own snark. "Not always. Only when I need to lighten the mood. And you can call me Javier."

She studied him for a second before she continued. "Okay." A pause. "Javier." Another pause. "I've been studying the video of the incident and your report. You knew what he was up to, and didn't stop him until it was almost too late. Why?"

Javier sighed. This was why the door was closed. Suvi had edited out her part in things, and otherwise modified the tape to read like Javier was controlling things.

But she'd left everything else as it had been, including his own compliance.

"Because I wasn't sure I was going to stop him."

He watched an eyebrow go up mutely.

"You people are pirates, lady," he continued. "There was a chance we could declare a medical emergency, suffer a couple of casualties, get the rest to medbay, and go from there. Make the galaxy a better place."

"Casualties," she chewed quietly on the word. "Who did you have in mind?" There were no doubts in her eyes, or her voice.

Javier stared at her for a moment, sighed. There was nothing for it. "You."

She nodded, minutely. For someone from *Neu Berne*, that was roughly the equivalent of Javier jumping up and down on the bed and howling various deprecations at the gods.

They both let the moment pass.

"What made you change your mind, Javier?" Her voice and her eyes were much softer now. Not nearly as hostile and agitated as he was used to from her. *Neu Berne* society. This had gotten to be far more personal than he had planned.

"You said please," he said, finally.

At her look of total confusion, he waved a hand. "I don't mean then," Javier said. "Earlier. Something minor and insignificant, I don't even remember what without looking through the tapes. It doesn't matter. You had gone beyond merely civil and were making an attempt to be nice. That mattered."

The look in her eyes was distant, glacial. *Neu Berne* society.

He watched her study him, really study him. The kind of closeness she hadn't bothered with at any point in the previous several weeks. It made him very uncomfortable, but he'd decided to come here, to do this.

"You could," she whispered, "have done something thirty seconds earlier."

Javier nodded. "Yes. I could have. And I could have also waited thirty seconds and shot him in the back with your gun. I'd like to think I made the right choice."

Javier keyed the door open and slid out as soon as it was wide enough. From outside, he gave her a grim grin that softened into a smile as the door closed. He would probably never again see her with her jaw slack in surprise. It felt good.

Be sure to pick up the other books in The Science Officer series!

The Science Officer
The Mind Field
The Gilded Cage
The Pleasure Dome
The Doomsday Vault
The Last Flagship
The Hammerfield Gambit
The Hammerfield Payoff

You can get volumes 1-4 collected together in
The Science Officer Omnibus 1

Volumes 5-8 are collected together in
The Science Officer Omnibus 2

ABOUT THE AUTHOR

Blaze Ward writes science fiction in the Alexandria Station universe (Jessica Keller, The Science Officer, The Story Road, etc.) as well as several other science fiction universes, such as Star Dragon, the Collective, and more. He also writes odd bits of high fantasy with swords and orcs. In addition, he is the Editor and Publisher of *Boundary Shock Quarterly Magazine*. You can find out more at his website www.blazeward.com, as well as Facebook, Goodreads, and other places.

Blaze's works are available as ebooks, paper, and audio, and can be found at a variety of online vendors (Kobo, Amazon, and others). His newsletter comes out quarterly, and you can also follow his blog on his website. He really enjoys interacting with fans, and looks forward to any and all questions—even ones about his books!

Never miss a release!
If you'd like to be notified of new releases, sign up for my newsletter.

I will never spam you or use your email for nefarious purposes. You can also unsubscribe at any time.

http://www.blazeward.com/newsletter/

Connect with Blaze!

Web: www.blazeward.com
Boundary Shock Quarterly (BSQ):
https://www.boundaryshockquarterly.com/

facebook.com/KRPBlaze

goodreads.com/Blaze_Ward

ABOUT KNOTTED ROAD PRESS

Knotted Road Press fiction specializes in dynamic writing set in mysterious, exotic locations.

Knotted Road Press non-fiction publishes autobiographies, business books, cookbooks, and how-to books with unique voices.

Knotted Road Press creates DRM-free ebooks as well as high-quality print books for readers around the world.

With authors in a variety of genres including literary, poetry, mystery, fantasy, and science fiction, Knotted Road Press has something for everyone.

Knotted Road Press
www.KnottedRoadPress.com